I0735622

Lethal Impact
Shattered Stars Book 2

By

Viola Grace

Used as a sexual trading card between the rich and powerful survivors of the lethal impact has left Fiona with an urge for change. She needs out, and the offer from an alien race to be a bondservant until she paid out her transport and training is an offer she wants to take them up on.

Once on the education base, she gets the help she needs to feel something again, and that training is going to come in useful when her test results come back and place her in an elite group of humans who can be of use to the Hmrain.

Aarak has just learned about the humans from his sibling, and as he was in the area, he decided to see if another human could be found with the high sensuality rating that his people needed to feed. He wasn't thinking of his people, he was thinking of securing a long-term bond mate that would serve him as he needed it. He could never have anticipated the wounded woman with a heart of gold who brought up instincts he never knew he had.

Lethal Impact
Published by Viola Grace

Look for me online at violagrace.com, Sea to Sky Books, Amazon, Smashwords, Kobo, B&N and other ebook sellers.

Chapter One

Fiona fought the rising nausea and pulled her shirt closed as she left the general's bed.

"Aw, Feefee, can't you stay for a bit? I am feeling inspired."

She shook her head. "No. I have to be back on duty tomorrow morning. I am working in the gardening centre."

He got out of bed and went to the bureau. "Well, here you go. I must say, I don't know where you put it all."

She smiled weakly and fought her shudder as he ran his hand down her spine and trailed a wet kiss across her lips. She took the month's worth of credit chits and smiled slightly at him before she took her leave.

Fourteen months of hell had locked her into the cycle of whoring for her boss. He had been a green senator, and she had been on her first day as his aide's assistant when the asteroid turned the world into a haze of cloud, ash, and static storms.

Her boss had died the day that the dust wave had hit them. Her asthma had locked her airways as it had so many others. The senators ahead of Senator Cormin had been killed in a variety of ways, and so she and her new boss had been shuttled into an underground facility to wait out the toxic storms.

In a very suspect decision, few—if any—families had been evacuated to the bunker. It was military men, politicians, and theoretical scientists trying to guess a way out of the eternal winter caused by the planet-killing asteroid.

With Fiona being one of the only

women on the base, sex had come into the equation at the six-month mark. Instead of trying to seduce her, they had begun to go to the senator who simply ordered her to their rooms at odd hours. When she hesitated, he fired her. Not having a job in the base meant that her rations were no longer a right. She had to earn them in other ways. She began to whore herself out to eat, and the senator offered to reinstate her, for a price. He connected her to the most influential of the men—she got protection during the day, and the price was a visit at night, once a week.

She had seen enough wrinkled skin to mentally craft an elephant.

"Did you get them?" The senator was waiting for her outside her room.

She handed over the ration chits, good for a lot of favours and more influence.

"You know, the line of men wanting

to get inside you is getting ridiculous. Some of your old favourites can't even make it to the list. You might want to start giving it away now and then, just to keep them happy."

He cupped her cheek, and she jerked her head away.

With a deep sigh, she entered her quarters and locked the door behind her.

She hadn't told him, but she was already giving it away. If her body were the price for a chance somewhere else, she would take it.

Months ago, a signal had come through their systems, and an invitation rang out for those who wanted to leave the dying world that they had been born on. The first round had left already, and Fiona was planning on being in the next batch.

Thanks to using her more obvious skills, she had gotten a breather and exo suit. She had a week of rations, and all she needed was to get to the doors and out of the base. Her pass had been paid for in advance.

Every kink, every role play, and every sweating body that she had lain under or over was etched in her memory.

She would be able to get to the rendezvous coordinates in three days. The big holding point was her ability to leave. If her guard changed his mind, she was fucked.

She headed to the shower and scrubbed herself from head to toe. The general wasn't a bad lover, but he was quick and lost his erection if he tried anything to make him last.

Fiona shampooed her hair and braided it tight. It would still be damp in the morning, but she couldn't stand to leave it loose if she didn't have to.

She looked at the shower stall wistfully and spent the same glance on the toilet. It was going to be rough in the wilderness.

Fiona headed to bed and forced herself to sleep. It was a skill she had learned over the last year.

Survival counted on her keeping her wits about her. The senator would have had her staked out while he collected funds and favours with a line spreading through the commissary.

He was trying to urge her into multiple partners, and that was why she was running. Now it was coaxing, but soon, it would be a command.

Leaving now was her best chance at something new—air she could breathe and food she didn't have to sell her body for.

She had a bright mind, an eagerness to learn new things, and here, her prospects were sliding backward.

Fiona had another year on her birth-control shot, and she had probably already picked up some kind of venereal disease that hadn't yet manifested. It would be astronomically unlikely for her to have come out of this mess without a problem.

Her body unclenched, and she dosed into a stupor. In the morning, she would make her move.

She spent her morning in the hydroponic centre, harvesting food and working with some of the other lower functionaries at the base.

At lunch, she mentioned that she was heading to her room, and she headed toward the quarters until she was sure she was alone, and then, she veered off in the direction of the public showers, grabbing her go-bag from the lockers and slinging it over her shoulder like a gym bag.

A relaxed saunter took her to the gates where Arthur was waiting for her.

To satisfy the cameras, she kissed him slowly before picking his pocket in the agreed-upon manner.

The passkey wasn't a key, it was a ratchet. She was getting out through the air system.

Fiona slipped the ratchet down her pants and smiled at the guard. She wanted to run, wanted to charge out for freedom.

Instead, she stroked her hand down his chest, caressed his erection through the fabric, and then, she headed down the hall to the access panel.

The ratchet took a few tries before she was able to pull the bolts and get into the air systems. She crept through the ducts with her bag on her back until she reached the filtering centre. This was the easy part. The codes to open the outer door were known to the high councillors inside the base, and she had slept with them all.

With swift punches of her fingers, she opened the door, slipped outside into the toxic air, and closed the door behind her.

Moving quickly, she changed into the exo suit and breather. Without hesitating, she ran away from the base as quickly as she could. When she knew she was lost in the grey dust and fog, her heart beat a little easier.

Behind her, she heard shouting and male voices calling her name. She charged into the dimness as quickly as she could, following the path laid out by the directional system.

Fiona had one chance to start over, and even death in the wastelands was better than life being used without thought for her in any way.

Circumstances had screwed her over, now it was time to take her own back. Her life was going to get under her own control, even if she had to sell her soul to get it. Freedom wasn't something she took for granted. She was willing to sacrifice some of it to gain control of her future.

She kept crashing through the dead woods and down the hillside until she was sure that they wouldn't follow. The wind blasted at her suit, pushing and pulling her with every step.

Fiona needed to hike for six hours to get halfway to her target destination. She was going to be sore when she reached the rendezvous.

Camping out in the wind and dust was difficult. She huddled against the trunk of a tree and covered herself with a thermal blanket. The few hours of sleep that she was able to get were all that she needed to get to her feet and march through the still grey air of morning.

Fiona stumbled through the ash and

brambles, sucking air through the breathing mask. She kept going, checking the compass as she went.

When she spotted the surprisingly new structure in a hazy meadow, she headed for it.

It was in the right direction, and at least it was shelter for a few hours before she continued again.

She stepped inside and was in an airlock. Through heavy, clear panels, she saw a variety of aliens and several humans. The humans were eating and getting some kind of scans.

At this point, the interior looked far more comfortable than what was howling outside, so she pressed her hand to the interior door.

A gas struck her from all sides, sending her senses into fight-or-flight mode. When the onslaught was over, the inner door opened and a man reached out to touch her hand. She flinched and pulled her hand away from the golden-skinned man.

He looked at her with soft amber eyes and smiled. "You are safe here. No one will harm you."

"Thank you. I am just... I would prefer not to be touched."

She recognized a few faces from the base, and to her horror, they recognized her.

Two of the men elbowed each other and smirked at her. The man speaking with her turned and eyed them. "Would you prefer to change in the privacy of a concealing curtain?"

"I have to change?"

"Yes, you will be given a shift and slippers so that all the med scans can be done easily."

She sucked in a deep breath and stiffened her spine. "Where should I go?"

He led her to an alcove and handed her a folded soft fabric with ballet-type slippers on top.

She stepped into the relative safety of the three walls. The curtain was slid across the opening, and it was time to make her final decision.

If she took off her clothes, she was peeling away her home, her family, ancestors, and all she knew. On the other hand, if she put on the shift, she would start with a clean slate. She had taken her clothes off for less potentially profitable reasons; before she could change her mind, her pack hit the floor, and her fingers went to the dirt-stained clothing that she wore.

The coveralls dropped, and her hands went to her underwear, unsure if they meant everything.

Shrugging she stripped completely. Standing with her feet on the cool, tiled floor of the prefab building, she took the shift and pulled it over her head. It fell to her knees and covered her completely. The slippers moved against her skin and snuggled into a comfortable fit.

Automatic slippers were a new one for her, but she ignored their movement and headed toward the medical area that had been pointed out to her.

Her metallic-gold alien came to her side and smiled, though the slits he had instead of nostrils were a little off-putting. "None of the scans will hurt, but some might tingle. Are you ready for them?"

"Don't you want my name?"

"Your name does not matter to me, nor mine to you. After you leave, there will be another human, and when you are on the station, there will be other guardians shepherding you. Remember them."

Fiona smiled slightly. "You are the first friendly face I have seen in a very long time. I will remember you."

"As you wish. Please, step into this

scanner, and we will begin."

She nodded, stepped into the machine, and settled into place as it began the scans. It was the most relaxed she had been since the impact. She was safe, no one could grab her, and for this one moment, her life was her own again. She fell asleep.

Chapter Two

Fiona woke up on a lounge with her golden companion next to her. "Sorry for falling asleep."

"It is understandable. Your scans indicated a state of exhaustion as well as several sexually transmitted diseases."

She flushed scarlet.

"Do not worry. They can all be easily treated; in fact, you are only two days from recovery. We administered the treatment. The concern is that there was quite a bit of internal tearing and bruising. You have been forced?"

She swallowed and looked out through the transparent walls to the men who were watching her and leering.

"Yes. I was not in a situation to support myself, so if I wanted to eat, I had to submit."

"Ah, right. So, no sexually based posts for you."

"No, please. So, how does this work? I had to get the information third hand."

He smiled. "Well, you sign an indenture contract, and the postings that bid on you will determine your final price. The job you are taken on for will determine the length of your indenture, and after that, you will be given citizen rights on the last world you were posted on."

"So, slavery."

"It is life. It is a life on a new world, with new species and a chance at thriving and, more importantly, surviving. The persons, companies, and worlds who are bidding are not charities. They are expending resources to gain personnel, and they must be paid in return."

"Do you work for a company?"

He smiled and nodded. "I am indentured to the education station. I work in assessment and examination."

"Ah. Okay. When does the assessment start?"

"It has already begun. You have administrative skills?"

"I do. Also, public speaking and customer service work is in my repertoire. In the past, I have been a pleasant person to be around."

"How are you with languages?"

"Fair. I can learn, but it is difficult to advance if there is no opportunity to practice."

"Excellent. That is what the scans indicated." He smiled, and his teeth were astonishingly sharp.

He leaned to one side and returned with a tablet. "So, here is a contract, written in your language, with a full explanation of what would be expected of you in your service. You have an hour to sign, or you will miss the shuttle, and this post will be moved elsewhere. You will be ejected and left to face your fate."

She inhaled slowly and nodded. "Right. Of course. I will have this done in a moment. Wait, can I sign addendums into the contract?"

"Yes, but it will limit your appeal to employers."

"I understand, but at no time do I wish to be sold by my contract holder or traded sexually."

"That is a reasonable request. May I?"

He took the tablet, and his fingers flashed over the screen. Under possible duties, the addendum had been filed.

She smiled slightly and kept reading. She could be expected to work up to fourteen hours a day. Clothing appropriate to her station and environment would be provided, as would food that she was capable of digesting. Her life would be hers to do with what she would the moment that she paid out her contract, which would include her purchase price, her education, and all medical care leading up to her debarkation from the education station.

There were other minor details, but it was enough for her to be able to control her sexual freedom to some extent. If they tried to bend the contract, it broke, and she was free as if she had gone through the entire payout period. In case of a broken contract on the part of her employer, she would be paid the entire cost of the contract and delivered to a world of her choosing within three systems. If she broke the contract by refusing to perform her job, she could be resold, and the contract term began again.

Fiona signed it. She had already seen the end of her world, why bother pretending that there was something better out there.

"Excellent. The other contractees are

a little too interested in you, so you will remain with one of us as an escort, and the station will know your situation before you arrive. Therapy may be involved."

Fee blinked. "Therapy? I thought you guys were here to sell us."

He scowled. "Of course not. You are a dying species on a rotting world. We are making a profit, of course, but you have a chance to go and live normal lives, as well as some of your kind, may choose to enrich other populations."

"You say choice like it is a real thing."

"When it comes to reproduction, it is. You will be given a fertility suspension when you arrive on the station."

She grabbed her arm.

"The one you had implanted was removed. You were growing scar tissue, and it would soon impede nerve function. The new treatment will have fewer side effects and will remain in your system until your contract ends unless you gain authorization from your employer to remove it earlier."

She blinked. "So, I am otherwise healthy? I mean, aside from the issues you have mentioned."

"Indeed. I am going to get your escort and settle you on the shuttle. As the first one on, you will be the last one off. It will keep you safer from those who seem determined to prey on you."

Fiona nodded. "Thank you. Ready when you are."

Her assessor smiled and helped her to her feet. He escorted her outside and into the shuttle, speaking softly with one of the crewmembers who was standing near the entrance. Their language wasn't clear, but the look of concern that the crewman gave her was unmistakable. He was looking at her with pity on his pale green features.

She was escorted to the front of the

wide chamber and settled into a chair. Her companion harnessed her in and stood at the edge of her row.

Five minutes after she had been settled in, the men from the shelter emerged in the ship and one, in particular, headed toward her.

Her escort stopped the man from entering her row and from sitting behind her. The man in the long smock scowled. "I have the right to sit where I want."

With carefully chosen words, her escort said, "That is true on your world. We are leaving your world, and from that moment on, you have no rights other than those that we have allowed you to have. Choice of position in a vehicle is not one of those rights."

One of the other crewmembers grabbed the human by his shoulder and sat him down near the rear of the vehicle.

Fiona wasn't smiling, she was nervous. That sort of man tended to use subterfuge and sneak attacks. She was going to need to be on guard when she reached the base.

One week and seventeen languages having taken up home in her mind, Fiona was feeling much better. She was in her general knowledge and etiquette course with other human women when one of the medical staff knocked politely on the door.

"Instructor?"

"Yes, Medic." The instructor paused her lessons.

"I require Fiona, Samantha, and Dione for assessment, please."

"Ladies, please go with the medic."

Fiona got to her feet and nodded politely to the instructor before she walked to the door.

The other two women joined her, and as a group, they followed the medic down the hall for whatever she needed them for.

"Please go with your attendant, and when your assessment is over, you may return to your class."

Fiona nodded. There was no arguing on the station. They had the right and the ability to fire you out an airlock if they wanted to.

The male attendants in the medical bay were waiting, and Fiona reached out to let the one with the scanner check the identification on her wristband.

The attendants were cream-yellow in skin with a slight metallic shine. Their faces all showed a focus on their purpose, and she couldn't help but guess that they were looking for something. Fiona went with the man who had her name on a clipboard, and he led her into the hive of cubicles without a word.

The comfy analyst couch and the small stool were strangely familiar.

"Please recline. Keep your clothing on. I will be touching your wrist only."

"All right." She settled on the couch, made sure that her skirt was pinned under her thighs and she leaned back and tried to relax.

He pulled the stool next to her, and he did place his fingers on the inside of her wrist. "Please, meet my gaze, and I will begin my assessment."

She looked into his silver eyes, and the world faded away. Fiona felt her blood rushing through her veins, pleasure, fear, every emotion ran through her.

Just as suddenly as the ride started, it stopped. Her attendant was sheened with the same sweat that covered her.

Fiona took stock of her body and felt the distinct pulsing of a faded orgasm along with arousal.

"What happened?"

He blinked slowly. "I took your psyche for a tolerance test. You have a high ranking, and it will remove you from the labourer class.”

“Oh. Right. Well. Good.” She blinked. “Can I return to class now?”

“You may return to the entryway. Your escort will take you to a different instructor.”

“Why?”

“If labour is no longer an option, you will need heavier protocol courses.”

She blinked. “Oh. Right. Thank you.”

He helped her to her feet and led her back to the front of the med centre.

“She will go into class one. The report is being filed.” Her attendant nodded to the medic who had escorted her.

The medic blinked. “Ah. Of course. Just a moment.”

She quickly spoke into her wrist unit, muttering about *a new one.*

“Wait here, Fiona. Your guards are on their way.”

With no other option, Fiona waited. Whatever was happening was out of her hands.

Chapter Three

The bond auctions were a secret, but they were also why Fiona had been tested so early.

It had taken her three weeks in her etiquette and language class, but she had finally gotten it out of her tutor. A human had been an ideal bondservant for a Hmrain, and that was a very big deal. The Hmrain didn't just own businesses or mines, they owned star systems.

Fiona's test had shown that she had the same capability for sensuality. She wasn't keen on that idea, but she had been assured that she was not going to be a whore. If she were a sexual bondservant, it would be to a single patron.

The counselling that she had gotten over the last few weeks had allowed her to make peace with that. She would have a place as a companion to her patron, see the stars, and enjoy herself until her contract was up.

If she did catch the eye of one of the rare Hmrain, she would have to deal with it, just as she would any other patron.

Oddly enough, she was not too worried about the likelihood of a Hmrain. The one that had gotten the first human was a fluke, and there were so few of the species that folks were lucky to see one in a lifetime.

Her tutor tapped on the desk. "Demonstrate the pour."

Fiona came out of her deep thoughts and poured the tea equally into the five cups, pouring once per cup and making each pour equal.

"Excellent. Do you have dance class

after this?"

Fiona nodded. "Yes. And defense class after that."

"Good. The next bond auction is in two days. Will you be ready?"

Fiona shrugged. "I don't know. I will be as ready as I can be."

"That is a very sensible answer. I am pleased with your progress, but keep your focus. The Hmrain are huge, powerful, and dangerous."

Fiona smiled as she tidied up the tea implements. "It is doubtful that one of them will appear if one of their kind has already been and gone."

Her instructor smiled. "A sensible conclusion."

Fiona got the feeling that she was being humoured. But really, what were the odds?

Fiona was hustled to the groomer a day early. She was taken out of her dance class and run through the scrubbing, bathing, oiling, and brushing with bizarrely intense haste.

No one would tell her what was going on, which was not unusual, but it was extremely annoying.

The soft blue gown wrapped across her breasts, snugged along her ribs, and then flowed loose. Underwear was not an option, but after a month at the base, she wasn't fixated on it anymore. Her periods had been halted, and with the shift, she had gotten used to the draft.

The dress flowed around her ankles, and the new slippers matched it precisely. With her hair pinned up away from her face and flowing down her back, she felt like everything was as under control as she could manage. Control was an illusion at this point. Nothing was happening as it should.

One of her guards collected her and gave her a small nod. "Your potential patron has requested that you join him for dinner."

"Um... okay." She looked around. "Where am I going?"

"Your escort is on the way. They will take you to the private chamber, and they will bring you back. At no time are you to engage in any intimacy with the Hmrain."

Fiona blinked. "It is not on my list of planned activities."

"Good. You will be given a full set of scans when you return to make sure that he did not overstep this privilege."

She inclined her head. "Of course."

"Remember your etiquette and training. Do not look at him unless he demands it."

"Right." She folded her hands in front of her and turned to face the guards that had arrived to take her to her dinner date.

Eight men and women of Grorian extraction were waiting. She stepped forward, and they surrounded her in a seven-foot wall of bodies. She had no idea where they were taking her, but they were doing it in state.

The Grorians were used around the base for the most exotic and important visitors. She had never heard of them being used for a trainee bondservant before.

The Grorians never failed to draw a crowd, but their retractable spikes generally kept the onlookers at a safe distance. Fiona felt very safe but very conspicuous.

The guards slowed, and she slowed her steps. Without a word, they parted, and she was left with one exit and one exit only.

Fiona stepped forward, and a host bowed low, motioning her to follow him through a private hall and to a large door. The door opened, and she stepped inside, joining the only other occupant in the space large enough for twenty.

"Well, you are quite lovely. That much matches the other one of your kind. Turn around, please."

She blinked, and her gaze slammed into his. Molten silver was the only colour that she could imagine. It was a high contrast to his rich green skin and complemented by the white of his hair and eyebrows. His wings were the same brilliant green, and she had to ask, "What did you say?"

He smiled slightly. "Turn around. I have never seen one of your species before, and I don't want surprises. If you have a tail, I would like to know now."

She turned slowly and felt a blush heat her skin. When the turn was finished, she resumed her submissive posture.

He chuckled. "Why do I think that that posture doesn't suit you?"

She flicked another glance at him. "I don't know. How much do you rely on instinct?"

He grinned. "I can observe, and what I observe is that being quiet and demure gets on your nerves."

She tried to look down again. "I have no comment."

He sighed and got to his feet. "Come here, little one."

His height was near to seven feet, and his wings arched above him, making him look taller. She tried to keep her gaze on his feet, but his torso was bare, with the exception of some glowing tattoos, and it was hard to look away.

"I am Aarak. What is your name?"

He took her hands in his and simply held them, letting the feel of callouses and rough skin sink in.

"Fiona."

He asked, "Would you care for a meal, Fiona?"

She blinked. "Yes, please."

"Allow me." He pulled her by the hands, and when she was near the end of the table where he had set up residence, he held a chair out for her.

She smoothed the gown around her backside and sat down. "Thank you."

"Thank you for joining me, though I am aware that you didn't have an option. I confess to extreme curiosity."

Fiona watched as he settled on a tall stool that left his wings free and clear. "Curious about what?"

He grinned. "About your species. I have taken the liberty of ordering for you."

"Thank you. I am still not accustomed to the variety of foods available here." She folded her hands in her lap again and looked down. All of the etiquette that had focused on meeting a nearly mythical species was suddenly making sense.

"While you are with me, I would ask that you look at me."

"It goes against protocol, sir."

"Aarak." He leaned toward her, and she could swear that he had the most interesting scent. She had shut her senses down, and her time on the station was helping, but he was the first male she was *aware* of.

She looked into his molten silver eyes and whispered, "Aarak."

"Better. Ah, here is your meal."

She turned and was shocked as half a dozen servers came in, each carrying a tray and eating utensils.

"Please, say I am not supposed to eat all of it."

Aarak chuckled. "No, but you must taste each one. I am trying to get a lock on your senses. Taste is the easiest calibration."

"I thought that this was just to interview me."

He cocked his head. "The interview was the light contact with your hands. Your body has tremendous potential, as does your mind. You simply need to feel secure enough to let yourself go."

She stared at the array of food that was arranged around her position in a semi-circle. "I have not been given the opportunity to give; the taking has always come first."

"Ah, yes. Your file indicated that you were used as currency."

She went pale. "Yes."

"That will not be the case in my service. If you are my intimate bondservant, you are mine alone. Your time will be yours when I do not require you. You may educate yourself, learn dance, art, language, or administration. You have a star system's worth of knowledge at your command." He smiled slightly. "When you are my bondservant."

She was stunned.

"Eat, eat."

She looked at the wide bowl she had been given and took a portion of everything, settling the food in an attractive manner before she took her first bite. She fought the smile. It reminded her of her favourite Indian takeout.

She ate a few more bites of two unimpressive offerings and then struck on something fun. A quick glance at her host showed that he was watching her idly, and there was a small smile on his lips.

"Why isn't my history an issue for you? Most males wouldn't want a female who had been handed around. I am damaged. Mentally, if not physically... anymore."

"They hurt you?" He frowned.

"Some of them. I was something to be used. Simply a convenience that they rented."

He nodded. "That will not be the case

in our situation, just so that you are aware. Yes, there is a strong sexual element but nothing deviant, and your pleasure is paramount."

She paused. "Why are you telling me all this? Don't you just bid on me tomorrow and then see if you are the highest bidder?"

Aarak smiled. "I wanted you to know that you have nothing to fear, and I wished to clear up a few things that were obfuscated in your file."

"Like my sexual history?"

"Like your ability to still feel pleasure. Based on your file, I wasn't sure if it was possible, though your assessment said it was."

She blinked. "Is that what that was about?"

"Yes. Sensuality level determines your ability to be an intimate bondservant. Your level is exceptionally high."

"So, I have been told." She sighed.

Aarak reached out and took her hand. The warmth from his fingers enveloped her and ran along her nerves.

To Fiona's shock, she started to get wet. Her pulse picked up, and she shifted in place. She looked at him in surprise, and he smiled.

"Eat your dinner, Fiona, and while you do so, tell me what wonders you would like to see."

She thought about what she wanted, and for the first time in a long time, she didn't feel desperate when she did so. As she ate, she told Aarak of her dreams of seeing the stars and learning what was out there.

When she had completed dinner, he helped her to her feet, kissed her cheek, and sent her back to her special quarters with her honour guard around her.

If he didn't bid on her after that, she was going to be pissed.

Chapter Four

The bond auction was nerve-wracking. Fiona was being kept for last, and she paced for hours before her turn was up.

Aarak was strong, imposing, but he appeared to be a male of his word. If she was going to end up having sex with one of the species of aliens she was compatible with, it might as well be someone who could keep up a decent conversation. Despite her internal assurances, she was also very sure that he was going to disappoint. No one that had ever come close to offering her freedom had ever *not* disappointed her.

"Come with me, Fiona." The Ymilian

woman with scarlet skin came into the room for the final time.

Fiona turned from her intense study of the wall, and she followed the handler out of the holding lounge and down the hall toward the bond auction.

"Step onto the stage and move if we ask you to." The handler smiled slightly, nodding her head as she withdrew from the pool of light.

It was like being in the weirdest high school play she had ever heard of. Fiona walked to the centre of the stage and faced the darkness where she could sense gazes trying to see through her clothing.

The descriptions must have been silent because bids began to course in. The number climbed, and Fiona got nervous. If Aarak was bidding, then someone was bidding against him, and that made her nervous.

She remained calm until the announcement pealed out. "Bidding closed."

Fiona looked toward the rectangle of light that appeared on the far side of the stage and followed the handler back into the light.

"That was exciting. Two Hmrain are never seen together, but here they were." The handler was nearly giggling.

Fiona clenched her hands together, and they shook while she followed the handler through the halls and toward the docking bay.

"You are to go with your patron and fulfill your duties until the end of your contract. He is in possession of all the details. Good luck, Fiona."

She could feel that she was white with panic, but this was what she had agreed to. She whispered, "Thank you."

The handler handed her off to two crewmembers wearing grey and silver. It didn't give her any clues as to the identity of her patron.

Protocol demanded that she didn't ask anything of the crewmen who were escorting her, so she had to wait until she saw the Hmrain who had possession of her bond.

There was one thing that she could be assured of, Earth was going to be a fading memory the moment that she entered that shuttle.

"Very funny, gentlemen." Four crewmen in green and silver appeared from around a corner, and they approached with fists clenched and their posture tense.

Her two guards halted and put a hand across the path through them. "We have been given instruction to take her."

"And you bribed the handler. This is not going to be well received. Aarak was the high bidder; he will have her. We have the contract to prove it."

Fiona backed up and got clear of the

crewmen in grey.

The collision of the crewmembers was violent, and the fight was short and brutal. The green representatives stood, and one bowed to Fiona. "Mistress, I have your bond contract, the proof of payment, and the name of your patron, Aarak."

She smiled. "Please, show me."

He lifted a tablet, and the projected contract with all the seals of the education station made her sigh with relief. "Please, get me off this station, and get that handler a short, sharp kick."

"That will be taken care of. Semak is filing a report right now." He smiled, his light mint features were shades lighter than his rich green tunic, the same colour as Aarak's skin.

"So, your colours are the same as the Hmrain you serve?"

He grinned. "You would have no way of knowing. Very nice move backing away. They were going to grab you and make a run for it."

"I guessed that when you showed up. Who were they working for?"

"Another Hmrain. Karus. He is a good sort, but his last companion passed, and he is looking for a new one. He arrived too late to introduce himself, so he decided to snatch you."

"When did you figure that out?"

"When Lord Aarak shouted in our coms and told us what was going on. He was very specific on outnumbering the guards of Karus. He was not taking a chance on losing you."

"I will have to ask him when he figured it out."

The guard chuckled. "That is your prerogative, Mistress."

As they talked, she was being marched to a shuttle where more green and silver uniforms were waiting to take them in and get them settled. The release from the station was smooth, and Fiona's skirt flowed up and away from her for a moment before the ship's gravity kicked on.

"We will be on the ship in twenty minutes. After that, we are heading home."

She inhaled and exhaled slowly. "Right. Twenty minutes, then a ship, and then a long ride through space."

"In the utmost comfort. Your wardrobe arrived with the other bondservants this morning, and you are the last passenger scheduled."

"Wardrobe?"

"Clothing, Mistress. You are coming to us with your skin and the gown you have on. Lord Aarak ordered a wardrobe for you, and it was delivered to his quarters this morning."

"Oh, I guess that is a good thing. Naked is not an option."

He gave her a strange look and shook

his head. "Yes, Mistress."

The rest of the twenty minutes were spent with her looking at the view screen and watching the huge shape of the wide and sleek craft that had to be the main ship get closer and much larger.

She fought the urge to hyperventilate as they pulled into the wide entryway that had opened for them. This was it. When the door to the shuttle opened, she was officially a bondservant. Of course, she was one now, but Aarak wasn't here, so it didn't count.

When her guard unclasped his harness, she did the same.

"Come along, Mistress. He isn't to be feared. He is not always kind, but he is fair. You have nothing to fear."

She wrinkled her nose. "You can smell it?"

"And see it. You have wadded your dress into a ball of creases."

He eased her out of the shuttle, and

her escort of four assembled around her. They began a comfortable pace through the ship and led her through an endless wave of corridors out and up.

When they reached a more formal area of the ship, she noted the security and the gazes that focused on her. She whispered, "Why are they staring?"

"They are looking at you, so you are recognized if they need to come to your assistance. As Aarak's personal guards, we need to know what you look like, Mistress. We can act as intermediaries with the other members of the population and guides when needed. Anyone wearing his lordship's livery is trustworthy."

"It is a nice thing to know. Are you also here to keep me from running?"

The men around her laughed, and her primary escort said, "No. If you want to run from his lordship, he will find you. There is nowhere you can go that he will not sense you and seek you out. We are just an interim measure to keep you safe from others. Your own impulses are your own business."

That was succinct, but it also made her wonder how many of Aarak's companions had made a run for it. The guards were aware of the possibility but knew escape was unlikely. That spoke of previous events. At least she knew that Aarak was fair. That was something.

He paused at the end of the corridor and bowed to her. "These are your quarters now. Knock and begin your contract."

Her guards melted back down the hall, and she turned to the plain metal door. She knocked politely, and the door opened, sliding to her right and leaving her framed in the opening.

"Come in, Fiona. I am very glad you made it. My brother has been chastised, and the handler has been removed from her position before she could leave with her bribe."

She held her breath as she crossed the threshold. The door closed behind her.

Aarak was standing near a desk and reading a complex visual display. He glanced over at her and smiled. "Welcome to the *Aura Breaker*. I have some business to attend to, and I know they didn't feed you, so the meal dispenser on the wall has a selection for you."

Fiona blinked. "Okay. Thank you, patron."

"Aarak. Don't make me remind you. You are the only one who gets to call me by my name, so use it." His tone was no-nonsense.

"You don't eat?"

He smiled. "We will discuss that later. Now, have a meal. You look positively grey."

She looked at the space that was twenty times larger than it would normally have been on the ship. "I will be fine. You don't mind my eating without you?"

His lips twitched. "No, while I can consume food, it is not required on a regular basis."

She didn't understand, but she nodded and went to the panel that he had referred to. Being busy seemed a better way to pretend she wasn't freaking out inside.

The dispenser had a smaller version of all the selections that she had had the night before. He had been paying strict attention. Only the foods that she had enjoyed were on the platter.

She held the platter and looked around, trying to find a safe place to set it down.

She saw Aarak move, and he stroked something on his desk. A table and chair emerged from the wall and slid into place near his desk.

"Have your meal here. This will be your study station."

"Study?"

"I have nineteen worlds under my care. You are my assistant and constant companion from this day forward. You will need to learn about them."

She blinked. "I have homework?"

"There is more to being an intimate servant than sex. You are my companion in all aspects of life. That includes my control and guidance of the worlds under my care."

The tray was warm, and she moved to set it down quickly. "I am not quite sure how this is supposed to work."

Aarak worked on a handheld tablet while the display fluctuated with weather patterns and topographical details. "It will unfold as we go along. The more duties you take on, the sooner you will be out of bond."

She snorted and started eating. "I saw

what you paid. I am going to be dead by the time I get out of bond."

"Maybe, maybe not. We will discuss that once we have consummated the intimate part of your bond contract."

Fiona focused on her meal and didn't respond to his absent observation. He knew something she didn't know, and sex was the price to finding it out. That was fine; she could do that.

The worst that could happen was that she would be in the same situation that she was on Earth, but only with one partner to please. How hard could that be?

<h1 style="text-align:center">Chapter Five</h1>

After her meal, she went exploring. Her wardrobe was next to Aarak's, and the bed was huge and self-explanatory. The bathroom was larger than the average one had been on the station, but then, the occupant of these quarters was not petite.

She was flicking through the entertainment options when Aarak paused, flexed his fingers, and turned off the display. "Apologies. Karus started a weather system on one of my worlds, and I needed to take steps to fade it out before lives were lost."

"He did what?"

Aarak walked toward her, and he caressed her cheek. "He was trying to distract me so that I would not notice that he had stolen you. My brother urgently needs a companion, but he cannot have mine."

His kiss was soft, warm, and remarkably chaste considering what it was doing to her body. Her pulse quickened, her vaginal muscles tightened reflexively, and she felt a flush cross her skin.

Fiona put her hand on his wrist, feeling the slow, steady pulse that was no indication of the effect he was having on her. He appeared completely unmoved.

The only points of contact were his fingertips on her cheek, and his lips, but she felt that she was at the mercy of escalating foreplay.

"Hop onto your desk, please, and raise your skirt."

She blinked in the haze of heat and did as he said. The first time with a lover was always awkward, so it was best to get it over with. She told herself that it was what was motivating her as she settled herself with her skirt raised.

Aarak moved toward her, and to her shock, he knelt in front of her. Her desk placed her at the precise height for him to lean forward and examine her private area in detail.

He didn't ask but gently raised his fingers to her, sliding two digits through her folds and pressing against her opening. His fingers dipped into her, and she inhaled sharply. He slowly moved his digits, testing her stretch. When he removed his hand from her and resumed his light stroking, his lazy exploration found her clit.

Fiona yelped when the zing of pleasure bolted through her. Aarak didn't smirk; he continued his investigation with thorough intensity.

Fiona felt her thighs clench, and he moved between them, holding her splayed wide while placing his lips against her opening. She fell back and braced herself on her hands as the silvery-white head licked and sucked at her while his finger taunted her clit until she let out a choked shriek as her opening clenched on his tongue. He switched the position of his fingers and mouth, flicking her clit while two fingers drove into her.

The hot burst of her orgasm continued on and on. She dropped to the back of the desk and twisted helplessly as the pleasure threatened to become pain. Fiona gasped and whimpered softly.

Aarak leaned back and slowly drew his fingers from her. "Your taste is astonishing. This explains Mero's fascination with his companion."

It was a fight to sit up from the prone position she was in, but when she was sitting, she watched as Aarak licked the last bit of her honey from his fingers.

The sight sent another tremor through her, and she cursed herself for being so easy.

He glanced up at her and smiled. "Don't worry about your reactions. I have many years of practice behind me, and as pleasure is my primary food source, it has behooved me to make sure that I am an excellent hunter."

He stood up and gently caressed her cheek once again. "We will get used to each other. I will learn you, and you will learn me. It is a fair trade."

She licked her lips. "It seems fair, but is it fair?"

He chuckled. "That will be for you to decide."

"And if I decide no, then I am still stuck."

He kissed her lightly, and she could taste herself on his lips. "You decided to pursue life versus death and a con-strained freedom over slavery. You can't have everything, but I promise you will have experiences that you never imagined."

He left her wet and rumpled on her desk, and she blinked slowly. She closed her thighs and went to the wardrobe on wobbly legs, grabbing a change of clothing before she went to the bathing room.

The sonic shower took care of the sweat and left her hair staticky. She found a brush set and got dressed in a simple button-front gown that had a fitted bodice but flowed around her feet. It was a rich green and black sundress.

She had forgotten to get slippers, so she wadded the auction dress up and looked around for the refreshing unit.

Unable to find what she was looking for, she came out of the bathing room to get some slippers that would match the dress.

"Did you get rid of the feel of my touch on you?" Aarak's voice was wry.

"No, I just got rid of the sweat and stickiness. And the fear sweat residue from the auction, and the panic from watching the guards come to my rescue. It isn't all about you, my lord."

She bobbed a curtsy and smiled as she met his gaze.

He laughed. "The dress looks good on you, but you appear to be looking for something."

"I was looking for the refresher unit, so I could put the bond auction dress in it."

"Take it back to the lav and drop it on the floor. There are bots that take care of it."

"Really?"

"Yes, they also change the sheets, make the beds, and repair damaged articles."

She looked around and didn't see anything. "Where are they?"

"They have cubicles in the walls and

emerge when there is no one in the room or on a schedule." He gave the shrug of someone who was used to the marvels of technology that he had access to.

She returned to the lav and dropped the gown on the floor. She backed away as far as she could and watched, but no bot emerged.

"They are not going to come out while you watch."

She wrinkled her nose and backed out of the small space. When the door closed, she counted to three and stepped toward it. The dress was gone.

"What the hell?" Fiona looked back at her patron with shock on her face.

"They are quick. They are designed not to get in the way." He gave her a sober glance from his silver eyes. "Now, come and start studying. We will be at our home before you know it. You might want to know what fruits and vegetables not to eat."

She sighed and headed to her desk, blushing as she looked at the surface that she had so recently been pleasured on. Aarak handed her a tablet with data on it, written in Heniahk. It occurred to her that they had been conversing in in that language since she met him, and she had been so struck by his appearance, it had slipped her mind.

The tablet showed her the planets that Aarak was responsible for, as well as their satellites, moons, and the uninhabitable planets in their systems. She gave him a dark look as she got to work. There was surely going to be a test later.

She yawned and rubbed her eyes. Her eyes burned, and her brain was numb after being bombarded with facts.

"If you are tired, go and rest. The only true rule is that there is to be no clothing in the bed. I require contact with you when you sleep, so please, honour this."

She blinked and looked at him. He wasn't leering; he was serious. She got to her feet and stumbled over to the bed, undoing each little button on the way. When she was down to the skin, she folded her dress and set it on a bedside table before she pulled the sheets back and crawled inside.

She hadn't slept the night before the bond auction, and her nerves were raw. Sleep came shockingly quickly.

Aarak's silver eyes were facing her when she woke. He was crouched next to the bed, and his hand was stroking her shoulder.

"It is time for dinner. The captain has invited us to join him. Please dress."

Fiona bolted upright and reached for the dress she had folded on the bedside table. It was gone.

"I will place your clothing at the foot

of the bed so that you may be properly dressed for my daily plans."

She nodded and ran her fingers through her hair. "Right. Of course, patron."

She looked at the dress at the end of the bed and raised her brows in surprise. It was similar to the one she had been wearing, but there were sleeves on the new one and a slightly thinner fabric. It would still be opaque but only just.

She flipped the sheets back and got up, stark naked and inches from Aarak. He smiled slightly and tilted his head.

"We shall repeat this moment after dinner."

She blushed but gathered her clothing and pulled it on. Slippers were on the floor next to her, and she stepped into them while she did up the two dozen fasteners. She was near her midsection when dark green hands pushed hers away, and she looked into Aarak's eyes as he slowly fastened her dress with his knuckles pressing against the inside of her breasts.

He smiled slowly. "You are very soft. I look forward to examining you at my leisure."

Her blush was going to be a permanent fixture, but at least the mottled green and black dress covered most of her skin.

"I will just fix my hair, and I will be ready."

"I am waiting." He flexed his wings, and for the first time, she realized that they were not ornamental.

Thinking about what it meant, she went into the lav and brushed out the marks of her nap, flipping the waves of hair over her shoulders. She stared at herself and lifted her left hand to tuck a few stray strands behind her ear, and she noticed the bracelet with the silver stone dangling from it at that moment.

When she emerged and went to Aarak, she held up her wrist. "What is this?"

"A bracelet to assist with locating you, and the charm will broadcast to your guard and me if you experience rage or panic."

She stared at him. "Why?"

He smiled and threaded a hand through her hair. "I find you attractive and utterly charming, but do not question me. You will do as I say without question, knowing that nothing I do will harm you, and keeping you sound is my fondest desire. Well, nearly my fondest." He smiled slightly, tugged her hair and then turned her with an arm around her waist.

She was reminded suddenly that this wasn't someone she could argue with, and he had a point. She didn't know anything about him, his people, or their traditions. Stepping out of bounds could be fatal if she didn't remember that he was her lifeline.

He walked her to the door and dropped his arm from around her waist. His wing extended out behind her, curving around her in a protective manner that managed to herd her in the direction he wanted without a word.

She kept her hands folded in front of her and walked with her head high. If this was her place in the universe, so be it. There was a number on her freedom, and she was going to find out what it was. She was more than a toy, and she would be in charge of her life again.

Chapter Six

$\mathcal{D}$inner with the Idel-born officers was astonishing. There was an equal representation of males and females at the table. The captain of the ship was male, but his first mate was actually his mate.

Aarak had his head turned toward the weapons officer, and they were conversing quietly, but on Fiona's left side was the head medical officer, and she had no interest in Fiona. She kept her conversation to her other side.

Fiona sat up straight and ate when the others around her were eating and drank when the others drank. By the fifth course, she was full. The foods were not sitting well, and she didn't want to stay still.

The green wine was having a strange effect on her senses. Everything was getting hot and then cool, and her head was spinning.

"Patron." She spoke softly, but Aarak didn't turn his head.

She slid her palm up his thigh, and he turned toward her with an astonished gaze. "I would like to retire. I feel very peculiar."

He gave her place setting a long look, and his eyes widened. "How much of the wine did you have?"

"My glass was refilled twice. Why?" Thoughts of poison ran through her head.

"Your system isn't able to process it. Doctor, I require your assistance."

The physician looked over with nearly a snap of her neck. "Yes, my lord?"

"You were in charge of the wine this

evening. Did I not make it clear that she was not to be served?"

The doctor gave her a contemptuous look. "It will not kill her, but it will provide you with much amusement for the evening."

He stood, sending his chair back with a clatter. "She cannot break it down. You have consigned her to days of torture. Captain, I expect you to carry out a suitable discipline, or I will administer it when we arrive at Idel."

The doctor paled. "It was a joke."

Aarak didn't comment. He reached down and pulled Fiona to her feet. Without another word, he led her out of the officer's dining hall and back to their quarters.

The world was hot and pulsing, or cold and echoing. Fiona had no idea what the next heartbeat would bring.

Aarak muttered and went to his desk. "I need the medic on duty, a scanner, and projector."

Fiona was standing in the centre of the room, shivering and twitching as her nerve endings were fired off in clusters at random points around her body.

Her patron returned to her, and he cupped her cheek. Fire burned through her in a very pleasant way, and she looked up at him with what she knew was a dazed expression. "Did she poison me?"

"She believed she was making a joke, but she did poison you. Idel consider the wine a light entertainment. It is relaxing and genuinely the beginning of a pleasant evening."

"An aphrodisiac."

"A mild one. A mild one in the Idel."

She fought the urge to put his hand on her breast or between her thighs. "Why didn't you warn me?"

"There should have been nothing to warn you against." He looked like he wanted to punch something, but his hand on her cheek was steady and relaxed.

The door opened while he stood staring into her eyes, and when the other person entered the room, he straightened. "She was given three doses of Mlia wine. Her system isn't designed for it. I need a treatment method to flush it out of her."

The medic looked a little flushed, but he nodded and gently eased Fiona toward the chair behind her desk. "How was the dose administered?"

"She drank it. It was served to her without my authorization and against my orders. It was a joke."

The medic gave her a concerned look. "How are you feeling, Mistress?"

"Hot, cold, aroused, dizzy, and my ears and vision make me feel like I am under water." She enunciated carefully because her tongue wanted to default to

English.

He pressed one monitor pod to her temple and one to a spot just over her heart.

While the monitors collected their data, the medic set up a display screen that projected her body in three dimensions, but it appeared that the focus was on her neural pathways.

A darker line was spreading from her abdomen and up toward her brain as she watched.

"So, that's the wine, huh?"

Aarak nodded absently. "Did you bring a unit with you?"

The medic bowed. "Yes, Lord Aarak. Do you wish to apply it?"

"I am not sure that it will work. You apply it."

Fiona watched as the medic opened level after level of his kit until he pulled out a layer covered with small electrode pads.

"Now, Mistress, these are going to bring you to a pleasure spike, as that does tend to burn out the wine rather quickly."

Fiona looked at him, and his appearance wavered in her vision. "I don't want to be touched. Just tell me where to put them."

"That will not be possible. There are some places that you can't reach, and to get correct placement, we need to compare it to your scans."

She looked over and asked quietly, "Aarak, would you put them on? You did say that no other person would be given full access to my person. I am not feeling up to being handled by anyone else right now."

Aarak looked at her, and a flicker of understanding crossed his features. "Of course. Please, remove your dress, and I will apply the unit."

She nodded and used clumsy fingers

to open the fasteners down the front of her dress. When it was open, she pulled her arms out of it and stood up. The fabric was left behind, and she braced herself on the desk.

The medic prepared the small stickers, and Aarak knelt in front of her, placing them as per the order of the medical professional, one at a time. The inner portion of her thighs got the small items as did every erogenous zone she had ever identified aside from the tips of her breasts and her clit. Even the back and side of her neck had small stickers applied.

Sixty small stickers were on her skin, and each had a tiny active unit within it.

"Mistress, please lie down."

Aarak nodded toward the bed. "Lie down, Fiona."

The medic followed her as she wobbled toward the bed, her skin felt like it was absorbing the little mechanical bits.

When she was reclining, the medic gave her a small remote. "Press this, and the units will calibrate. After they are quiet again, a single press will bring you to a slow climax."

"How will I know when the wine is out of my system?"

"The display's dark lines will fade, and your normal display will be reported to our office. The medical officer on duty will come and retrieve the equipment."

She pressed the button and asked, "How long will this take?"

"I will have a better idea once I know what progress a cycle has gained."

Each tingle of muscle and tissue fired up, and she saw a hot pink pulse on the display across the room.

The medic looked back at the display and then glanced at her in alarm. "Are you in pain?"

"No, it feels quite pleasant. Like I am wearing a TENS machine." She smiled as each nerve cluster was woken in turn.

It took several minutes, and Aarak lounged at the end of the bed, watching her twitching progress.

"Okay, now for the real thing. No offense, medic, please, stand near the display. I don't like to put on a show."

The medic flushed a darker green again, and he retreated to his equipment.

Aarak smiled slightly. "I am curious to see if this works. I know it works with Idel physiology, but it has never been tested on your folk."

She hit the button and held her breath. "No time like the present."

The electrodes started a light caress, and she lay on the bedding, shifting slightly as the caresses got stronger. Hands gripped her breasts, her body tensed, and desire roared to life.

She heard the medic speaking frantically, but the roaring in her ears blotted him out. Her arousal climbed higher, filling her with desperation. She twisted, and tears seeped from her eyes as she waited for release. Even stroking her clit had no effect. Her body wouldn't let her orgasm.

The stimulation from the unit slowed and faded. Fiona rolled over, and she sobbed. The fire in her blood was still ablaze, but she didn't know how she was going to end it. She looked at the other two through the cage of her arms.

The medic was now chalky pale. "Okay, so that doesn't work. I don't know what is an option. I need to check with the officer."

Aarak nodded. "Please, do that. In the meanwhile, I will try to assist her. You are dismissed now."

The medic gathered his equipment and left the scanner behind.

Aarak removed his trousers, and he crept onto the bed next to her.

Fiona looked at him and licked her lips. If anything was going to help, it was going to be direct contact.

"I am very sorry; this is not how I wanted to properly begin." He rolled her onto her back and kissed her softly.

She leaned up to taste him, and he flicked his tongue into her mouth. She couldn't define the taste of him, but she wanted more.

Fiona slid her hands over his chest, ran her fingers around to the base of his wings and down to his buttocks.

He shifted over her, and she felt the head of his cock against her, pressing into her hot and wet flesh. She rocked her hips toward him, and he eased into her. With a sigh of relief, she took him as deeply as she could, using the flats of her feet on the sheets to push upward.

Aarak shook and drove into her; he thrust several times before she felt another point of contact on her clit. She groaned, and sweat coated her while he stroked in and out of her with deliberate force.

It seemed rude to scream in his face, but she let herself relax and react, and after several minutes of battling for release, it struck her like a bolt of energy firing every nerve and neuron.

Aarak moved with slow and steady beats of his hips, keeping the pulses firing in her body.

Fiona groaned and relaxed under him, letting her lower limbs resume normal positions while she threaded her fingers through his white hair.

"So, will you look me in the eye now?" Aarak chuckled.

She glanced up and met his gaze. "It is a hard habit to break."

"Consider it an order. I can live for a year on the energy you just produced, but I would enjoy it more if I could see it when the pleasure takes you over."

Fiona blushed and then gasped as he kissed her deeply. She shivered and closed her eyes as she tightened her fingers in his hair and held on. The kiss was hot, slick, and caused her hips to shimmy against his.

He was still hard. He was also incredibly deep. When she moved her hips against him, the fire started again.

She whimpered and held tight to him as he shifted his hips slightly, and the suction on her clit resumed a throbbing pull. Slow motion inside her and the pressure on her clit were a deliberate tease that mixed with the taunting thrust and slide of his tongue. She was surrounded, filled, and overwhelmed by someone who was paying attention to every moan and twitch.

He broke the kiss and feathered his lips over her forehead while his hips moved slowly, pulling her slowly toward another orgasm.

The feeling of being cared for, cher-
ished, and watched was intoxicating. He
was taking care of her and learning her
habits. When her soft moans and shivers
overtook her, she met his silver gaze
while her inner muscles clasped him and
milked him.

He smiled at her and said, "How do
you feel now?"

"I have gone from scalding hot to a
low simmer. I need to ask a question."

"There is no better time, Fiona."

"Do you come?"

He grinned. "Yes, but today is not
that day."

"Am I going to have to do more reading?"

He laughed and slowly moved off her.
"I am afraid so. Once you have learned
about the Hmrain, I will fill in the gaps."

She fought her wobbly limbs and got
her legs together, sitting up and sighing.
"I thought that is just what we were do-

ing."

His grin was wide, white, and showed her some very serious fangs that had escaped her notice until then. She looked at his green skin, glowing silvery-white tattoos, the thick expanse of his cock that had had two-thirds of itself inside her if the gleam of her moisture was any indication, and gave herself credit for not running screaming into the far edges of the spacecraft.

<h1 style="text-align:center">Chapter Seven</h1>

The display showed a slimming of the dark lines, but they were still exceptionally thick.

Naked and sweaty, Fiona looked at the image of herself, and she cleared her throat. "So, that looks like it is going to take some doing."

Aarak wrapped his arms around her from behind, and he pulled her back against him. "I am willing to put the hours in, but it will injure you, so I will consult a specialist."

"There is a specialist?"

He sighed and rubbed his chin on the top of her head. "Sort of. The creature who designed Mlia berries projected its effect on other species."

"Creature."

He squeezed her. "My sibling."

"Your brother?"

"No, one of my sisters. Her ability to tinker with biochemistry is astonishing. She might be able to work out a solution for us. Do you mind if I share the particulars?"

"Since it is starting to hit me again, I would ask that you consult whomever you think can help. It is interesting right now, but if it doesn't wear off, I think I would end up a little depressed."

"Right. Did you want to rest?"

She chuckled. "No, I am rather energized. I think I will sit up and read about the Hmrain if you don't mind."

He slowly released his hold on her, and she walked over to the wardrobe, slipping on one of the robes she had noticed earlier. It was a strange combination of silk and lace, but she enjoyed the feeling against her skin. She took her tablet to the couch and recreational space in the entertainment area. Curled up in a corner, she listened to Aarak as he spoke softly to someone in a language she hadn't heard before.

A woman's voice countered in the same language, and she seemed amused.

He asked a question, and she answered with one word. He argued about that word, and she reiterated it. Finally, he shut the connection down and leaned back, fuming.

She glanced up from the article that described the Hmrain penis as *an adaptable appendage.* "You look irritated."

"I have gotten an answer, and it is not the one I wanted."

"No help with the prognosis?"

"No, I have been given a treatment option. I just don't want to administer it."

She set the tablet down. "What is it?"

"I am not going to do it, so there is no point discussing it."

Fiona got to her feet and walked over to his desk. She turned him away from the screen and opened the robe so she could straddle his hips. He sat back in surprise as she traced her fingers over his tattoo.

"Now, tell me how to stop this overtly annoying behaviour, or I will seduce you." It was an empty threat. His body was hard and ready for her.

She wrapped her hand around him and stroked his erection. It grew even thicker in her grip, and she wondered how she had gotten it inside to begin with.

His eyes narrowed, and he hissed. "What is fostering this confidence?"

"Check the display."

He glanced and gripped her arms when he saw what she had noted. The dark streaks were thickening again.

"How are you so calm?"

She met his gaze, and his look of understanding let her know that the churning maelstrom of desire was visible in her eyes.

He slid a hand between her thighs and found the slick heat that she had been trying to ignore. "You should have told me sooner."

"If I had told you sooner, you would still be inside me. It hasn't let up; it just receded in urgency. So, tell me how the Hmrain eat pleasure."

He thrust two fingers into her, and she rose on her knees. "The Hmrain have adapted to consume the pheromones and brainwaves of our partner and transfer them into a radiation that our bodies use as an energy source."

She shuddered as he thumbed her clit. "So, do you go through many women?"

"Women, men, anyone who can rank over two hundred on a sensuality assessment is a suitable source of energy. Of course, I can also draw power from populations in my vicinity."

She was losing track of the conversation, but she had to ask, "What happens with a rating under two hundred?"

"The source dies. I drain them."

She shivered. "Oh."

"Indeed. Place your hands on my shoulders."

She quickly did as he said, and he leaned forward, grazing his sharp teeth against her neck. Fiona gasped and tilted her head to one side, enjoying the flicker of pain.

He gripped her hips and lifted her, settling her on his cock. He didn't give her any warning, he simply pulled her onto him, eliciting a sharp inhalation of breath and a whimper.

She looked at him, but he was exposing his teeth and heading toward her breast. She closed her eyes and winced at the light prickles of pain that preceded the strong suction on her nipple.

He pulled her onto him in a slow thrust that ached as much as it sent pleasure through her. It set a pattern of pleasure and pain that struck all of her sensitive areas with him using teeth, tongue, cock, and fingers to elicit the responses.

He didn't seem to be encouraged by what he was doing. In defiance of their earlier banter, he was sullen and determined as he fucked her. Her body's reactions swelled toward orgasm. It didn't care.

When she spasmed around him, he bit into her neck, and her grunt of release turned into a shriek. The sensations mixed and melded until she was throbbing from head to toe.

Tears rolled down her cheeks at the

realization that this was going to keep happening until she had worked the toxin out of her system.

He withdrew his teeth from her shoulder and licked softly. "I apologize, but the pain was necessary. Look at the scan."

Sniffling, she turned her head, and the dark lines had receded and thinned. "You could have warned me."

"It would not be as effective. The panic and fear that ran through you worked to cancel out the effect of the wine."

She blinked, and through the aches and pains, her lust was definitely diminished.

"I do feel better."

"Good. Take a bath and rest. The bath will soothe your muscles and give you a better idea of your state of mind."

She leaned back, wincing at the pressure in her womb. "There is a bath?"

He looked surprised. "Yes."

"With water?"

"Yes. It is recycled once used, but it will last us the next week of travel."

She put her hands on his shoulders and tried to lift herself off. "Help please."

He chuckled and used his hands under her thighs to move her off his cock. He got up himself, letting her know how strong he actually was. He was carrying her like she weighed nothing.

He walked with her past the display, and the lines were continuing to shrink. That reminded her. "I am covered with electrodes, can they get wet?"

"They can, and we will remove the small stimulators. They don't do you any good and make it hard to lick you in long passes."

She blushed at that. "Right. Will you help me get them off?"

"I will. Sit at the edge of the tub, and

by the time it has filled, we should have found them all."

Fiona nodded, and while he fiddled with the taps, she started to rip off the tabs that she could reach. She had managed twenty of them by the time Aarak returned.

He helped her remove the rest, including the ones on her inner thighs. The short flares of pain as they came off could only help her at this point.

"On your belly so that I can reach the others."

She gave him a dark look, and he went over her from neck to the soles of her feet, collecting all the tabs in a small pile.

"There. Let me check, but I think we have got them all."

She grunted and got to her feet, the hot water calling her. She held her arms out at her sides, and he ran his hands over her from neck to feet slowly and thoroughly. She sighed. "Can I have a bath?"

He pulled a single tab from the back of her knee. "Yes. Now you may. The other monitors are long term and able to submerge, or I will just put on new monitors." He smiled brightly.

She stuck her feet into the water and smiled at the warmth of the climbing level. When it reached her groin, she winced. As the water climbed, she felt every inch and every deliberately rough caress, including the finger in her ass. The pain flared as a living reminder for an instant before the water made the sensation a distant memory.

When she was finally in and settled, Aarak cocked his head. "May I join you?"

"Please." She leaned against the edge of the tub, which was more hot tub than bathtub.

He entered with a wave and splash,

completely at ease with his nudity.

"What happened to my robe?"

"On the floor next to my desk. It got in the way."

She chuckled and leaned back, closing her eyes and listening to him get settled and shut off the water.

"How are you feeling, Fiona?"

She glanced at him with a smiled. "Sore but better. Thank you. I know that it wasn't part of your plan to spend an evening using sex as a medical treatment."

"I did not want to see you suffer over the course of days, and I wasn't sure what the effect of the Mlia enzymes would have on your brain."

"Well, there was a weird euphoria. I felt elevated, sexy, and irresistible, but it was the feeling of having a fire at my back that was going to consume me if I didn't have sex immediately. It was less than pleasant."

"Not a great first day."

She laughed long and low. "I had forgotten that. No, not a great first day. Tomorrow will be better. At least, I am not afraid to jump you when the mood takes me."

He sighed. "The idea is that you are available when the mood takes me, but I do not mind servicing you as you like."

It was a bit of independence and aggression that she wanted to experience, and he knew it. She could exert her personal power as much as she would like, as long as it matched with his plans.

The partnership that was forming between them was weird, but since they were both learning the other person, the steps they had made felt huge. As she let the water soothe some of her aches, she smiled; she had definitely learned a few things.

Chapter Eight

$\mathcal{P}$anic swelled in her chest, and her heart beat in a staccato stampede as she woke with a warm body in bed with her.

Aarak kissed her shoulder. "You will get used to it. This is only your third morning on the ship. When we are at one of the bases, and you can have a proper schedule, it will be easier for you."

His arm was around her waist, and his grip kept her flat against his chest and thighs. With his wings, he could only sleep on his side or his belly, so he ended up spooning her through the night. It was fine when they collapsed together in a sweaty heap, but she was always alarmed in the mornings.

"One day you will have to tell me what happened, you know." He feathered kisses along her neck.

She shivered and sighed as she shifted to give him a full range of touch. "I do feel better having those monitors off."

"I regret that it took so long to purge the Mlia."

She shrugged. "It's over, and it isn't as if there wasn't pleasure in with the pain. I am just not a fan of a few of the places you chose to inflict it."

"I will make the discomfort a distant memory. So, are you up to eating in the galley this morning?"

She sighed as he patted her belly. "Sure. Just let me zip through the sonic shower, and I will be with you."

"You have a strange obsession with cleanliness." He sat up and ran his hands through the mass of his hair that was not confined by neat metal bands.

She rolled out of his reach and walked across the room to the lav. It was a major triumph that she could now go to sleep with him after sex. It was a two-night habit that she hoped she could get used to. The first night, she had lain awake and passed out when he left the bed to attend to his business, but the second night, he had had shocking sex with her until she had finally dozed.

The night before, he had been tender, and she had slept easily in his arms. Waking up was another matter, but she hoped it would get better in time.

She took her quick sonic shower and brushed her hair. She smirked. He had braided the hair from her temples while she slept. Fiona brushed around the long braids and headed into the living quarters to go to the bed for her daily assigned gown. After the first night, nudity was no longer an issue. His tongue had been in and around most of her already, so he knew what she looked like.

One of the officers was standing next to his desk when she emerged. She shrugged mentally and kept walking. Aarak was still naked, and it wasn't as if it was a mystery as to why Fiona was there.

She hummed to herself as she picked up the dress, and she slipped it on and fastened the dress up the front. The front opening was Aarak's favourite, so it was what she was wearing. The shoes matched the dark silver gown.

When she was dressed, she smiled at Aarak and went to her desk to take up her daily assignment. The day before, she had been learning about the evolution of the Idel people, and now, she had to find the turning point of their society, somewhere in twelve thousand years of history.

"Fiona, what is your thought of our

journey extending slightly by a detour to one of my worlds?"

She inclined her head. "Whatever you like, patron. Everything here is new to me. As long as I can breathe on that world, I am happy."

He nodded. "You have your answer, Lieutenant. We will divert to Ekadi."

The officer nodded, bowed, and left their chamber.

Aarak stood and stretched. "So, are you ready for your meal?"

She chuckled. "I am, but you might want some trousers or a wrap or something."

He looked down and shrugged. "The Hmrain are not that fussy about clothing."

She grinned. "I noticed."

He smirked and went to the wardrobe to get his own clothing for the day. He put a pleated skirt on that draped from each knee up to the waist, and a central panel hung to his knees. It reminded her of Egyptian images she had seen as a child.

"Ready for your meal?" He smiled, his silver eyes sparkling.

"I am."

She stepped to his side, and he extended his wing. This was his preferred method of protecting her in the halls, and protocols were what he whispered into her ear as she was falling asleep. *Sexy pillow talk.* She smiled as they exited their quarters and headed to the galley.

The Idel crew stood aside and let them pass when they ran into them in the halls. It was not worship, it was respect, but Fiona hadn't run into that part of their history yet.

"So, what is on Ekadi that you have to take care of?"

"There is an issue with their harvest. One of the naturally evolving creatures requires half of what the locals plant, but they do not wish to part with it.”

“Will they starve?”

“No. They have plenty of reserves.”

“Is it migratory?”

“No, the animal rises once every century and needs the food to spawn the next generation.”

“There is only one?”

“For now. There has never been enough food for it to spawn and survive.”

She frowned. “If it is only every hundred years, why are they kicking up a fuss?”

“This generation has never seen the beast. They have studied it via cavern excavations, but they have never looked it in the eye or seen it fly.”

She blinked. “It flies?”

He smiled softly. “Oh, yes. It has been several risings since I have seen it, but it flies.”

Fiona mulled that over and entered the galley with him. He directed them toward a high table and helped her to her seat.

His chair was the thinly backed style that made it comfortable for his wings, and he settled his elbows on the table. "Do you have thoughts on the matter?"

"Not until I can read more on the subject. It isn't my place to meddle with other civilizations."

"Your place is what I say it is, but it is wise of you to wish to research the event. The odd thing is that they celebrate the day with a festival. They always have."

The galley head came to their table and bowed to Aarak. "What can I get for you, my lord?"

"A meal selection from species level six for my companion, and two glasses of water."

The crewman nodded and scurried away.

"How long has their species been on the planet?"

He cocked his head. "I believe it has been eight hundred years now."

"So, what happens to the parent when the offspring is born?"

"They have three years of flight around the world, developing, and then, they burrow into stone, and the count begins again. The parent never emerges after that. They simply give themselves to the stone that sheltered them, I suppose."

Fiona bit her lip. "I guess that finding out what happens to them after their natural life cycle is complete would help to determine what would happen next. Do you know what the effect of the flight is? When the hatchling and adult fly around the world?"

"They alter the wind patterns and the harvests for the years they are flying, and the crops are always abundant as if making up for taking what they need."

"That seems more than fair."

"I believe it as well, but I have to make my presence known on the surface to drive that point home."

Her meal arrived, and she sat back while the hot stew and wedge of bread were slid in front of her. It smelled fine.

"I know I can eat it... by why level six?" It was a genuine question. Humans were level three.

"This is the style of food that was served on Ekadi when I first arrived."

She tasted the stew and analyzed what she was eating. There was a meat, a starch, some bright flickers of vegetation, and more starch in the form of the bread. This was farming food. The folk who ate this had no time for anything fussy. "This style of food didn't originate in a lush valley. This is subsistence-level food."

She continued eating because breakfast was breakfast.

Aarak tilted his head. "How do you know that?"

"One-pot meals like this are for folk who are busy with other things and who need food that can cook unsupervised."

He appeared impressed. "Very good. Yes, they were an agrarian culture."

"And you met them and introduced them to the valley, and they all came along to build new lives."

"Correct."

"And they developed their technology at an alarming rate that has produced a population who believes only in what can be measured and quantified."

He frowned. "How do you know that?"

"It explains the contempt of the natural world. I am guessing that it is the same on many planets. You feel that you are in control of your environment, so anytime it does something you don't like, you are furious and seek to quell the offshoot of unpredictable activity."

He nodded. "My people have observed the same across all of our worlds. Some species gain the wisdom with the technology, but others simply want to rush to an ending that they cannot predict."

"Yeah, I am aware of that last one."

She finished her bread and stew and drank some water.

"So, tell me about your life after the impact on your world."

Fiona cupped her hands around her water glass, and she told him about being in the wrong place at the right time and hauled away to safety with the politician she had been assigned to.

The early days when their survival was not assured, she had stuck close to her employer, and then, the barters had begun.

She had been offered a better place to

sleep than the open barracks, and she had paid the price, not knowing until then that her employer was coming along for the ride. She paid for everything with her body, and the more that they could get from her, the less that they offered.

"When they asked for oral sex in exchange for coffee that everyone else got for free, I began drinking water. When the communal desserts were offered in exchange for hand jobs, I stopped eating sweets. Everything that everyone else received free and clear, I was expected to pay for. Toward the end, the only thing that I paid for was my meals. The moment there was anywhere else to go, I escaped."

His eyes widened. "I am amazed that you agreed to the bond agreement."

"The initial assessor entered the paragraph into my contract that I would only have to serve one person if it was in an intimate manner."

"Where is your joy?"

She paused and stared down at her hands before looking up at him. "My family is dead, my world is dying, I have no home and no place in the universe. I don't mean to sound depressed, but I have no joy. I have existence and survival. I am content with that."

His expression was appalled. "That is not life."

She wrinkled her nose. "No, I suppose not, but I am hoping that as I travel, I will regain those moments that make life fun again."

Aarak gave her a grim expression, but there was a twinkle in his eye. "I believe you have just offered me a challenge."

She hadn't felt this nervous since she decided to run for the stars.

Chapter Nine

"I haven't taken you on a tour of the ship yet." He mentioned it casually as they walked the halls.

She shrugged. "We have been busy."

He sighed. "Yes, that. Did you want to learn about the punishment given to the head of medical?"

"No. She acted in malice, and as long as she isn't able to do it to me again, I am fine. Mlia wine is off my items to try now."

He chuckled. "You are wise beyond your years."

"I am wise based on my experience. I have just had more of that than most."

"True enough. What did you want to

be before the cataclysm?"

She wrinkled her nose. "A florist. An organic farmer, I wanted an apiary. All of those occupations took a short, sharp shock and stopped at the strike. When the world broke, so did my dreams."

He let out a grunt and turned to lift her. "That's it. You need a distraction."

She thought that it was supposed to be her job, but she didn't say a word. He walked swiftly through the halls, and she smelled greenery. A door opened, and she gasped at the forest and farm that was laid out in front of her.

"We will get a better view."

It was the only warning he gave her as he crouched and launched them upward. She shrieked and wrapped her arms around his neck as his wings flexed and scooped air out and down.

Fiona finally opened her eyes and looked around, seeing upper levels and the forest below. "You generate oxygen here?"

"Not really; it costs more than you would imagine keeping the plants whole and active, but it does provide a morale boost to the crew. They have concerts in the gardens, most of the fresh food is grown here, and it provides a reminder of Idel."

She smiled as she saw some of the variety of skin tones that she associated with Earth. "How many humans did you bring on board?"

"With yourself counted? One hundred and twelve. They seem to be doing well. They are relieved to work in the gardens."

She chuckled and held on as he flew them lower, across the fields. "It was the first thing we lost. Stored food only lasts so long, so getting hydroponics up and running was imperative. I volunteered for that job, but my skills were needed elsewhere."

He let out a sound that she interpreted as a growl. He pulled them upward and wrapped his wings around them while he let the ship's gravity pull them down.

Fiona was secure in his embrace, but she squeaked in shock when she counted the seconds, and they were nearly to the ground.

His wings opened and billowed back behind him as he caught them inches from the soil.

She smacked him on the chest as he settled down on his feet. "Thank you for giving me a heart attack."

He laughed. "I was after distracting you."

"It was effective." She was shaking, but there was a giggle in her mind. The inner chuckle shocked her. If she had to have near-death experiences to make her snicker, she was going to die laughing.

"Would you like to speak to some of your people?"

She tensed. "No, that won't be necessary."

Aarak frowned. "Why not?"

"Sexual prudism is a common theme in Earth cultures."

"But... they used you."

"It is also a highly hypocritical societal construct. Males are encouraged in sexual promiscuity, but women are villainized for it. It puts us in the lowest social class, and there is no way out once you are in it."

He wrapped his wing around her, and they began to walk toward the exit. "So, when you said there was nothing for you..."

She moved toward him slightly. "It was exactly what I meant. They would not allow me to have a place among them if they knew what I was doing after the impact and definitely not if they knew I was your intimate companion. I would be contaminated beyond measure."

"But, the folk here do know."

Fiona looked up at him. "Are you going to make me live with them?"

He frowned. "Of course not. You will remain with me at all times."

"So, it isn't an issue."

"I suppose not, but I thought that seeing your people would make you happy."

"Seeing the plants makes me happy. Let's stick with that. Tell me about the trees and the bushes."

He took her on a tour of the Idel plants, and the head horticulturalist was only too happy to show her the leaves and tell her about the root spread and growth schedule. She lost her mind in the details of the plants, and for a short moment, she was happy.

She was examining a short berry bush and turned to grin at Aarak. His surprise made her laugh, and the horticulturalist was shocked when his lordship caught her up in his arms, and he flew her up to their living level.

His flight had crewmen and women hitting the deck to get out of the way, and by the time he had landed in front of their quarters, she was pretty sure what had lit his fire.

He didn't make it inside. He pressed her against the wall and shoved her skirt upward. She gasped at the feel of his cock pressing into her, but it narrowed to enter her and thickened once it was inside.

He held her and stared into her eyes, not moving his hips.

Confused, she frowned, but soon, his cock began to twist and rub inside her, and she stared into his eyes in shock.

She sighed, whimpered, and clung to him with all her strength as he took her higher than she had been with him before his cock sent out the attachment that stimulated her clit.

She shrieked as it sucked and pulled hard at her, her body shook, and she clawed at Aarak, trying to gain purchase on his impervious hide. Her channel clutched at him in spasms as she met his gaze, as per his demands.

The molten silver of his eyes went dark, and he began to thrust his hips into her, rubbing her against the wall.

He paused and shook his head, his gaze returning to normal. He leaned in and kissed her softly, still deep inside her.

She was dazed, a little bruised, and utterly perplexed.

Aarak wrapped her in his wings so no one could see any part of her, and he walked the few steps to their quarters.

Once inside, he walked to her desk and set her bottom down on the edge. Still, without speaking, he knelt in front of her and spread her legs wider, he leaned forward, and his tongue slid into the wet and swollen space his cock had just been in, and she whimpered as it thickened and twisted around inside her.

His hands wrapped around her thighs and held her still when she tried to back away, but she was locked in his grip while her senses pushed her higher and higher.

Fiona jerked, moaned, gripped, and let go of his hair, shivering and finally flexing her hands in frustration as she lay back on the desk with nothing to hold onto.

The tension burned in her, and when she couldn't hold back any longer, she screamed and clawed at the desk.

He kept his tongue moving against a sensitive spot inside her until she was dizzy. Fiona slumped back, exhausted.

She was still dressed, coated in sweat

and panting for air. Aarak pulled his tongue out of her, and he stood up to cover her.

He whispered against her lips. "You need to laugh more."

She tasted herself on his mouth and blinked. "If I do, you might fuck me to death."

He grinned. "Never to death. I swore to uphold your health, and I will do it."

"Before or after you wear out my lady parts?"

He laughed, and she smiled. It was nice to see that he was happy that she had been happy for a moment. It had been swamped by panic and confusion, but the happiness had been there.

"Fiona, take a quick shower and get changed. We will be landing on Ekadi in two hours. You will need to learn what you can about their traditions and situation before we set foot on the surface."

She nodded and tried to get up. "Um,

you are in the way."

"I have your juices all over me. A shower for me is a good idea as well."

She yelped as he lifted her and carried her into the lav. She leaned against the wall while he unfastened her dress and removed her shoes.

"I can do this myself."

He shrugged. "I chose the dress, so I will remove it. While my wrap was convenient, it is not suitable for the Ekadi weather."

She grinned. "Too drafty?"

"Quite."

He turned on the sonic shower and turned her, making sure that the dirt on her skin was vibrated into the suction unit. He treated himself to the same situation, and she realized that if she got to the wardrobe, she could pick her own outfit. With a grin, she dashed out of the lav and through the living quarters, pausing only when she saw the long-sleeved dress and boots that were waiting for her next to the bed.

"Oh, balls." She slumped her shoulders and dragged her feet toward the bed, picking up the very pretty dress in rich green, black and silver, and pulling on the soft black boots. The laces on the boots needed to be tightened, but once they were, it was like wearing a very comfortable pair of long socks.

The dress was in the standard configuration of being a long coat with a series of fasteners that closed it between breast and knee. The fabric was light, but it still felt weird not to have any underwear on. The dress flowed around her and touched the abraded front of her thighs. As long as she wasn't standing on a glass walkway, she was modestly dressed.

Aarak wandered over to the wardrobe, and he pulled out a pair of snug trousers, some black boots, and a black vest that was split to allow his wings to settle neatly around him. Watching him get dressed was always fun. Everything went from the bottom up to be settled into position.

He tightened his boots and turned to her. "How do I look?"

She sighed. "Very pretty. Just a moment." She walked over to him and straightened the line of the vest before adjusting his banded hair to fall forward while the rest draped down his back. "There you go. Very nice and rather dignified."

He frowned. "Your hair came undone."

She blinked. "It is fine. I just brush it and let it go."

"No. Sit on your desk."

She looked over at her desk and frowned. "I am a little nervous when you say that."

"Good. Now, put your bottom on that desk and wait for me."

She sighed and went to hop up on the desk. She sat and swung her legs as she waited. He disappeared into the lav and reappeared with a brush and some of the same kind of clips that he wore. It was a cross between a metal bead and a small tube.

To her bemusement, Aarak brushed her hair, separated the two locks over her temples, and rapidly braided them into columns held with the beads.

He set the brush down and smiled. "There. Now you are appropriately dressed as my mate."

She smiled back as she hopped to her feet and took up her tablet for more study with her butt appropriately on her chair. She was into the stories of the Ekadi arriving on their word when her brain processed what he had said. *Mate?*

Chapter Ten

$\mathcal{F}$iona's first steps on an alien world were not graceful. The wind that struck her and sent her skirt whipping around her legs made it hard to focus.

Aarak pulled her close and provided a windbreak at her back. "It is better near the city."

She smirked. "I am just glad that the fastener goes as low as it does."

He grinned, lifted her, and flew them both into the city where a large crowd had gathered.

The people of Ekadi were elegant, willowy, and had a smug sense of self-satisfaction that Fiona wanted to smack off their lips.

Their elected representative met Aarak, and the three elegantly dressed women behind him bowed low.

"My lord, I am surprised that you have bothered yourself with such a trivial matter." The official waved his hand at the women behind him. "We have prepared an offering for you."

The women smiled and swayed toward him. They paused a few feet away and curtseyed so deeply that Fiona could see they engaged in complete landscaping, the view down their cleavage was impressive.

"We are at your service, my lord." They even spoke as one.

Fiona looked up to Aarak, who was still holding her. "You are not going to fall for this, are you?"

He smiled and shrugged before setting her on her feet. "You may need a rest."

"Like hell." She turned toward the offerings that were nearly a head taller than she was. "Your services are not required. Shoo!"

There was no word for *shoo* in Ekadi, but the women frowned and tried to go around her. It was a mistake.

Fiona kicked the legs out from under one of the ladies, punched another one in the nose and grabbed the third by the hair, pulling her to the ground by use of her green locks.

"Do not touch him, do not coo to him, do not think to come near him. He is not yours." She growled it, let the woman go and stood straight.

Aarak wrapped her in his arms, and he apologized. "My mate is a little territorial. Where may we speak about the rising?"

The official stared at Fiona as Aarak lifted her off her feet and carried her into the tent that had been set up for the purpose.

The official waited until Aarak sat down on the specially designed chair with a fuming Fiona on his lap, and then, he took his own seat.

"The archaic practice of tithing to the creature is over. We are an intelligent people, and we do not need to placate an ancient god."

Fiona snorted.

The official cocked his head. "You find something amusing, madam?"

"We have not been introduced. I am Fiona."

"I am Master Hedding."

"Of course, you are."

"You did not answer me." He looked offended, like an irritated forest elf.

Fiona looked at Aarak, and he grinned. "Go ahead, you did the research."

"So did you, that is how I knew what to look for."

"Go ahead, Fiona."

She sighed. "Right, so the creature comes out every hundred years like clockwork."

"Correct."

"It eats half the harvest of the valley."

"Correct." Hedding looked irritated.

"It flies around the world for three years and returns to its home."

"Correct. This is common knowledge."

She smiled tightly. "Then, you know about what it does while it sleeps?"

He looked wary. "It sleeps. It hibernates."

"It releases three years of food altered by the digestive process into the soil of the valley. The first burst of food lets it fly, and the rest of the time it goes looking for enough food to have an offspring that would double the fertility of your area."

"No, that can't be it." He frowned and pulled out a tablet.

"Your land yields less each year following the rising until it returns. It is not a superstition, it is biology and horticulture."

Aarak kept his hand wrapped around her hips. "That is what I have come to tell you."

"Why didn't you mention this earlier?"

"It did not come up. I usually amused myself with your welcoming committee." He grinned.

"Yeah, that isn't going to happen again." She elbowed him in the ribs.

"Of course not. Now that I have found you, I no longer need to dip into other species."

She frowned. "I have other questions for you."

He grinned. "I will answer them in our quarters."

Hedding cleared his throat and asked, "Do you mean that our civilization is built on a manure pile?"

Aarak shook his head. "No, it is dirt. The soil is enriched at a much lower level. Have you already seen the signs of the rising?"

Hedding shook himself out of his amazed confusion. "It will rise by dawn tomorrow. We didn't prepare the offering."

"You had better get to it, or the creature may not return. No return means that your valley will lose nutrients and fade away."

Hedding bolted to his feet. "Please excuse me."

Before Aarak could dismiss him, he was out the flap of the tent.

"Well, I have achieved what I wanted; do you wish to return to the ship?"

Fiona wrinkled her nose. "I would rather have a look around and see some of the city. I have never seen an alien world before."

"All worlds are alien to you, as you are alien to them. Excellent attack sequence, by the way."

She twisted her lips. "Yeah, how did I manage that?"

"You nap a lot, and I thought it a waste, so I have given you some subliminal courses."

"Self-defense?"

"Nothing so useless. No, you have bar-brawling skills based on the Idel bodies and movements. It is a fairly close match."

"Speaking of matches, why me? Why not one of the Idel who follows you with sad and wistful eyes?"

"I would kill the Idel. Besides, they are all vaguely related to me, so it is slightly perverse to think about."

"How so?"

"Another question for the ship."

She elbowed him again.

"So, would you like to see the city?"

"Yes. Yes, I would."

He looked down at her with raised brows. "Would you like to see the creature?"

She nodded. "Please. If it is going to wake up tomorrow, I would like to see it just this one time. I won't be around the next time it flies."

"You will outlive your lifespan. I am quite sure of it." He grinned, and his wings parted the closure of the tent before they were out in the sunlight again. He smiled, lifted his face upward, bent his knees, and shoved hard against the ground while propelling them into the air with great scoops of his wings.

The drag of gravity kept her tense and curled against him until they were at the altitude he wanted. When the pressure eased, she was able to look up and around.

"Holy heck. This is a crater."

He grinned, and their path took them

toward the outer rim. "You are very well informed."

"I couldn't see it from the crop-level images in the file, but this is an impact crater. Something struck this world with enough force to displace all this soil."

"Correct."

"Did the creature come with the asteroid?"

He shook his head and smiled ruefully. "Yes. The Ekadi have a revisionist view of the universe. I barely fit in it, but they certainly didn't want to believe in beasts with no names that lived in the stars and planted themselves into worlds until they were ready to return to the stars. Ekadi is a nesting ground, but the creatures give more than they take."

"I get that. I wonder if the rock that hit Earth had something living in it."

"It will take a century before it would wake if that were the case. If there is one, it will spend its first years clearing the skies of the dust and debris. After that, it will find a nesting area near its crash site and go dormant again. What would your folk do to it if there was one?"

She didn't need to ask. "Kill it. They would blame it for the destruction and kill it while it slept. That is if they could get close to it."

He nodded. "That is my guess as well, and what I was afraid the Ekadi would do. So, when I led them here to this crater, I told them that the creature was mine as well. They didn't dare go after it in the first few centuries when I was living here, but after I left, they began to grow irritated with the thought of sharing their bounty. Now, they are finally mature enough to understand the symbiosis that they are living in."

Fiona thought about where humans had been a hundred years earlier, and she could see the difference that the years would make. "Time makes all the difference."

"It truly does. I am delighted by how quickly you are catching on."

She smiled at the slight insult and watched their flight path take them along the edge of the rock face. There was no indicator of where the creature was, and the moment that Aarak pulled in his wings and clung to the rock with one hand, swinging her into a slight crack in the wall, she realized they had reached their destination.

She looked up at him and could only see the silhouette of him with the halo of light behind him. "Is this it?"

He laughed and helped her to her feet. "It is narrow, but it is here. Follow the path of warm air."

She stepped into the darkness, and as she slid her foot forward over and over, she felt the sides of the cavern, and when her eyes adjusted, she could see a light in the darkness.

"Is that it?"

"It is. It glows. It is the originator of some of the radiation that runs through my own veins."

She looked back at him and could make out his features. The band of tattoos on his upper arm and the one across his chest were glowing, and it seemed that they were pulsing in turn with the light ahead of her.

She turned to face the growing light inside the tunnel, and she whispered. "It pulls the rock in when it sleeps?"

"The radiation melts the rock into a natural-looking formation. Unless you know what you are looking for, you will never find the entrance."

Fiona stepped toward the light, and when she reached the edge of the path, she gasped. Under her was a creature that was breathing so quietly that only the shifting of its skin gave away its activity. Twisting curves of patterns that looked like burns but went into the hide and not upward covered the exterior edge of the glowing cream-coloured hide.

"Is this the only colour?" She crouched to get a better look.

Aarak crouched next to her. "It will darken and take on the radiating colour of the spectrum. When light touches it, it becomes something much more fantastic."

"Will we stay until it flies?"

The creature shifted slightly, and Aarak tensed. "I think we don't have long to wait. Quick. Back the way we came."

She was on her feet and moving with him at her heels. When she would have spilled out of the cavern, he grabbed her, pulled her in tight, and jumped off the cliff edge.

His wings bellowed wide, and he

gained altitude once again.

In the distance, at the edge of the enormous crater, was the city. The locals were working outside of their city limits. Fiona hoped that they were preparing the food.

They had just reached a height that was endangering her oxygen when Aarak whispered, "Look."

She looked down at the stone ridge where they had just been skulking, and the rock blasted apart in an unceremonious explosion. It was as if the cap had been ripped off the ridge, exposing the creature below.

The two hundred metres of creature stirred and slowly began to lift upward. The flat teardrop shape lifted, and as it rose out of its nest, feathery leaves unfurled around the surface, and it lifted out of the nest and took to the sky.

"Holy hell, why is it coming this way?" Fiona was shocked as the creature came directly toward them.

"It wishes to greet us; hold tight."

Fiona quickly wrapped her arms around his neck and did as instructed. What followed was an aerial waltz of loops, bows, and twists above the surface of the crater. The huge creature matched them roll for roll. It seemed to know the dance and was comfortable with its size in comparison to the Hmrain.

Fiona was shocked when the dance ended, and Aarak landed on the creature's back. "What are you doing?"

"It wishes to take you on a ride. It is happy I have found a mate."

She blinked. "It said all that?"

"In the twists and rolls. It got a look at you and asked me what you were, so I said you were my breeding partner, and it asked if it could show you its territory. I agreed, and here we are."

Fiona looked around, and to her

stunned amazement, she was standing on an alien creature that hibernated every century, holding the hand of another alien that she couldn't even guess the age of, and being shown a world that was in the early stages of development but still more evolved than her own. It was a very interesting way to spend her day.

Chapter Eleven

$\mathcal{T}$he VIP quarters were wide and spacious. Fiona twirled happily through the room while Aarak had a meeting with Hedding.

The food was being spread out for the creature, and it was already beginning to feed.

Fiona replayed the view from above in her head as she sat on the edge of the bed. It had been incredible. She had felt the care and concern that the creature had felt for the land beneath it.

This world was about to bloom, and the creature's work over the centuries was about to pay off. Caches of the incredibly strong fertilizer were about to activate, and the development of the world was going to go from a walk to a gallop.

The crash site of the Ekadi was also one of the areas on the tour, and their pathetic civilization had been shepherded to this place where they could survive and thrive. Their response was turning into one that she was all too familiar with—if you don't understand it, kill it.

Food was sitting on a sideboard, so Fiona got to her feet and nibbled at bits of the offerings, waiting for any side effects before continuing on. When she was full, she walked back to the bed and laid down. Her guards were outside the door, and she was safe to simply rest.

As she felt the cool bead against the side of her neck, she smiled. If that little braid weren't there, her hair would be even wilder than it was. Aarak had surprising domestic skills.

She wondered if he could cook.

* * * *

The attendant retreated after verifying that his lordship's woman was asleep.

She immediately passed the guards and headed down to the meeting hall where Master Hedding was meeting with Lord Aarak.

She rushed into the room and paused, walking calmly toward the man she dreamed of. "My lord, your companion is asleep. If you desire anything, I am here to serve you."

He glanced at her with his devastating eyes, "No, thank you. My mate has me satisfied for the first time in my life."

The maid stumbled. "I heard you could never be sated, my lord."

"I couldn't, and for her, I am not. No other women can gain my attention now, for, with her, I need hold nothing back. I can take my fill, and she can take more. Frankly, it is wonderful."

The maid blinked.

He smiled kindly, "I appreciate your offer, but if I had need, I would simply have to touch her cheek, and she would roll over to receive me. I have finally found someone I wish to keep at my side. I wish you to find yours."

He rose to his feet, inclined his head to Hedding, and headed for his temporary quarters and his mate.

He passed the guards that he had assigned to her and entered the room that was only just large enough for comfort.

Fiona was curled up on her side, facing the door, fully dressed with her shoes on. He grinned and walked up to the bed, removed his clothing, and cuddled against her on his side.

She curled against him and pressed her hands to his chest. The smile on her lips warmed his heart as she settled into a deep and restful sleep.

He could have chosen a mate with more exotic features, but he never could have chosen a better one for him. He was lucky that he had made it to the station in time. The thought of her with another one of his kind turned his stomach.

Aarak wrapped his left wing around her and held on tight. He wasn't risking his treasure.

* * * *

The Ekadi bathrooms were a little odd, but she managed to do what she needed to in the morning. She had a shower and then got into her dress from the day before.

Aarak had woken before dawn to engage in more meetings with the Ekadi. Fiona got dressed and looked out the window where dawn was peeping, and the creature appeared in the light, heading toward the city. As Fiona watched, the creature got closer, the huge fronds undulating as if it was under water instead of breathable atmosphere.

Fiona stood in the window and watched the approach and was stunned as the creature came to a halt with one frond held down to the window while the others kept it aloft.

"You want me to climb that?" She blinked slowly.

The creature didn't say anything, but it remained in the locked position.

Jumping onto an alien wing six stories above the ground wasn't something she would have normally done, but she felt a pull in her mind that promised joy and tranquility, and she had to respond.

The first step out of the window was the big one. When she landed on the frond, it curled around her protectively, and she was able to scramble up and onto the back of the creature. The wind tugged at her skirt and hair, but when she managed to get midway into the frond, it folded upward and deposited her on the heavily grooved back of the creature.

It turned and flew away from the city. From down below, Fiona could hear exclamations, and with a final look over her shoulder, she saw her guards in the window of the guestroom, staring helplessly.

Wherever the creature wanted to take her, she was going for the ride. She really wished she had had breakfast.

The creature flew for hours at an astonishing speed. Fiona held on to the grooves of the markings when she needed to, but for the most part, she was able to lie on her back with one hand over her head for stability and watch the sun trying to catch them.

Stars were poking through the lightening sky, and it was amazing to her that she now had confirmation that some of them had people on them. The humans of Earth were no longer alone, and some of them were heading to the stars. It was a heady thought.

She laughed. She was in the stars. It was still so hard for her to understand. She had survived the worst that nature and humanity could manage for her, and now, she was on the upswing across the universe. Well, she supposed it was true. *Location, location, location.*

The creature began to slow, so she rolled over and looked at their destination. Soft sand had slid down a hill, and an exposed rock glowed green with a soft pulse.

"I think I can see what you wanted me for." She sat up on the creatures back, and when she saw the stiffened frond, she headed for it.

The dress wasn't exactly made for

climbing, but she made do. When she was on the ground, she made a run for the crystal and scooped the sand away from it, grabbing it with both hands and hauling away.

The rock tingled in a way that told her it probably wasn't the greatest thing for her to hold onto. Regardless, she worked the rock free of the sand around it, and then, she raised it above her head.

To her surprise, the creature didn't take it; it turned and offered her *two* fronds. Catching on, she put the crystal on the left frond, and she clambered up the right. By the time she was on the back, the crystal had been nudged next to her, and she took the hint. This was hers to protect until they got back to wherever she was being taken.

The creature turned and headed back the way they had come. Fiona exhaled in relief and watched as they flew back toward the city.

A dark speck in the sky turned into Aarak, and she was surprised when they crossed each other, and he didn't make it onto the creature's back. He stopped, turned, and followed them, growing closer minute by minute.

He was nearly to them when the creature slowed, and he overshot them. They were near the valley, and she reduced her speed until she was barely moving. The hint was there, so Fiona grabbed the crystal and slid down the frond once again. Fiona walked in front of the creature with the crystal; she centred it and then put it in the grass before running out of the way.

During the trip, she had gotten flickers of the idea of what was going on. Aarak flew up to her, grabbed her, and hauled her into his arms while he got away from the creature.

"What did it do?"

"She. She needed help and thought

that because I was your mate, I would understand."

"Did you?"

"More or less. Enough to get the job done. Watch."

The creature lowered herself over the crystal, and its colours began to change and flash wildly. Fiona clapped her hands in delight. "She did it. She has been trying for centuries, but now, she did it."

"Did what?"

Fiona leaned on his shoulder as he climbed higher to keep his distance from the creature. "She got pregnant. The next time she rises, there will be two of them, but first, she has to eat."

He frowned. "I thought she needed food to reproduce."

"She does, but the crystal is one of her eggs. The images I got were scattered, and I have quite a headache now, but she needed a woman to collect the egg because she wanted a girl. Every time a man finds a crystal, they have touched it, and it turned male, which means that it would fly as soon as it was grown. This world needs more work than that. It needs another keeper, so the child will take this on as a nest and the mother will move on, and they will meet every hundred years."

She sighed happily and leaned against Aarak. "It is sweet, really."

"It can be sweet, but we are leaving. She will be fed, her people will leave her alone, and you and I will return in a hundred and three years to meet her daughter." He kissed her forehead.

"I will be dead by then."

He snorted. "No, you won't. You might even have a child of your own to show her."

"I used to dream about being a mum." She was dozing from the stress of the day.

"Did you? Well, we can hope." He pressed another kiss to her forehead, and he flew directly to the area where they had landed their shuttle.

He kept her in his arms in the shuttle, and her guards were giving her dark looks. She sighed and settled in Aarak's arms, confident in her good deed for the day.

<h1 style="text-align:center">Chapter Twelve</h1>

Her first three days on Idel filled her with a question that only Aarak could answer. "Why do they hate me?"

He looked up from his desk and blinked. "What?"

"The Idel. I haven't met one that is pleasant to me, and I don't know why. Well, the guards have been pleasant, but then, they are paid to be nice to me."

He frowned. "I will have a word with Miskaro."

She winced at the name of his butler. "I am sure that will go swimmingly."

He leaned back and groaned, stretching his arms up, and she watched his chest as it rose and fell, the muscles flexing.

"Come here, Fiona, and I will tell you of my relationship with the Idel."

He patted his thighs, and she smirked but walked over and straddled his thighs. She opened his trousers and settled herself over his cock and waited.

"When I first met the Idel, they were young but had potential to be great. I left and returned a few hundred years later, and plague had ripped through the citizens, leaving only a few thousand survivors."

She felt the stirring under her, and he opened the closure of the top of her dress and pressed his lips to the top of each breast.

She wove her fingers through his hair, and she moved his head to her nipple; he didn't hesitate to suck strongly at her, running his tongue along her skin before pulling at the other nipple. She shivered and felt the wet invitation that she was issuing against his cock, and his flesh eased into hers, pressing upward until it could go no further.

He lifted his head. "To foster survival, I gave them my blood. It changed them from pale yellow to the soft green and made them my family."

Her eyes went wide as his cock churned slowly inside her, rubbing all the nerve endings and causing sweat to trickle down her spine.

"So, I am not good enough for you."

"Something like that. They want me to choose one of them, but I would kill them. I would drain them in moments. Each generation thinks that they are the one for me, and I must decline them all the time."

She started to rise and fall against the twisting inside her. "So, what have you done to feed yourself, Aarak?"

"I have used my hunger to punish the guilty and dispatch those with a death sentence."

She would process what he said later, for now, she was focused on the wet slap of bodies striking and the heady feeling of enjoyment as she approached orgasm. His hands gripped her hips, and he started to thrust into her.

She felt her release come and go. He lifted her and laid her back on the desk, pressing into her and pulling nearly all the way out before surging back in. He pounded against her and then held himself tight while he groaned.

Fiona held onto him as he shook and bucked into her.

The door opened, and she heard a voice. "My lord, there is a visitor for you... oh, do excuse me."

Fiona didn't bother looking at Miskaro. Her attention was fixated on the shocked expression on Aarak's face. She could smell the musk and feel the extra moisture seeping out of her. It was definitely a new sensation.

Aarak looked at the intruder, and he shouted, "Out!"

Fiona was held in place by his weight. His hips twitched, and he shuddered a final time. "Easy, Aarak."

Flickers of pain began to make themselves obvious. Her neck ached, her breasts were sore, and there was a deep-pressured throb inside her that was going to be there for a while.

He looked down at her, and his expression was bewildered. "That should not have happened."

She stroked his cheek and ran her thumb over his lower lip. "It happens. It doesn't matter. I am birth controlled within an inch of my life."

He frowned. "I think my body forgot about that."

He was still inside her, but she decided that she had his full attention. "Did my post-Ekadi scans ever come back?

That was quite a bit of energy in that stone."

He cocked his head. "Come to think of it, no. I am going to withdraw now."

She stroked his cheek again. "Thanks for the warning."

He kissed her softly and pulled out, leaving a trail of strangely warm fluid on the inside of her thighs. She was pretty sure it was semen, but Aarak was green, so she was slightly leery of the sight she would face during cleanup.

He helped her sit up and fastened her dress again. He licked her shoulder and the top of her breast. "I didn't mean to bite."

"I didn't notice. Well, now that you have tucked yourself in and I am relatively decent, I believe you have a guest?"

He nodded. "Please, open the door."

She walked to the door and swung it open. "Miskaro, he will see you now."

He walked past her, and his expression was prepared to say something snide, but his nose twitched, and he bowed. "Thank you, mistress."

She was stunned. She returned to the desk and chair that Aarak had had installed in his office, and she tried to get back to her studies.

The head of medical from the ship charged in, waving a report. "My lord, she has been contaminated by radiation."

Aarak looked over to Fiona, and he smiled as if sudden understanding was washing through him. "Has she?"

The physician paused and inhaled, stopping sharply before turning to Fiona. "You are in..."

The medic rifled through the reports, and the slick sheets fell from her fingers.

Aarak smiled. "Let me guess, she is in heat. The radiation is benign, but it has altered the mechanical arrangements that she had initially."

The medic nodded. "I was going to say she is dangerous."

"I would say so; she is triggering my rut early. If all goes well, there will be another of my kind here in the next two years." He cocked his head. "I wonder if it will be a son or a daughter."

The medic went from pale green to blue to a weird grey.

Fiona murmured, "I think you can go now."

The medical officer literally ran out of the office.

Aarak nodded. "The information has come late, but it is not unexpected. There was a reason that the creature made you hold the crystal for hours when it could have held it as well."

"Well, she did think that I was sick. That came through."

"Did you understand what was said?

"My birth control has been nullified,

and I am fertile, which is setting you off. Sorry." She grimaced.

"Don't be sorry, I just wasn't expecting this for a few more years." He smiled. "If you quicken, we will welcome it. But, in the meantime. I have found an occupation for you."

She leaned forward eagerly. "What?"

"Magistrate for your people. They are getting rather anxious and irritating the other species that make a home on Idel."

She nodded. "Right. What am I allowed to do with them?"

"You are going to keep them alive, right?"

"Of course, but I have not made it through the bondservant regulations for Idel."

"Ah, let me send them to your tablet. Can you begin tomorrow?"

"I can try." She winked. "As long as I get some sleep tonight."

"I make no promises, but I promise to

mutter regulations into your ear as you doze off." He winked in return, and the mood in the office was jovial if not anticipatory for the rest of the day.

Fiona was never going to admit it, but the change in her chemistry after Aarak's donation had done wonders for public relations with the Idel. They were polite and civil to her now. It was a nice change.

Twenty humans were milling around the magistrate's office, and when her guards parted them, she heard the sneers before she saw the faces.

She took her seat on the elevated chair and looked at the tablet on the equally high table next to her.

"Excuse me." She looked at the gathering, and they were ignoring her. *Right.* Fiona reached into the pouch she had brought for just this purpose, pulled out the polished orb, and she smacked it down onto the table with a loud *crack*.

All of the heads turned toward her.

"Right, we are here today to address the issue of nine counts of refusal to do assigned work that falls within the terms of the contracts, three petitions to begin a human neighbourhood within the city, and two requests for dismissal of the bond."

One of the men that she recognized said, "Where is the freak in charge?"

"Ah, you mean Lord Aarak? His is the name on your contracts, and you owe him for getting you off the station and onto a world where you can breathe actual air again."

Corporal Wellin smirked. "Of course you would say that. You are getting off easy, and a lot from what I hear."

She was expecting that. She looked around and addressed the group. "So, you are all aware that I am the intimate bondservant of his lordship?"

Smirks filled the room, and several women looked revolted.

Fiona cocked her head. "Who among you chose to be either labour or domestic bondservant? You got to pick your assignment, of course."

The smirks faded a little.

"Let me just lay it out. I did not choose this, nor did I choose the life that I ran from. Your bonds have definitive endings. You know when you are going to be released. I do not have that luxury. I have a bond so expensive that I would have to live to be over a hundred and fifty and acting as a magistrate that entire time before my bond was paid. I don't get to go free. I go where he goes, travel where he travels, and sleep where he sleeps. That is the situation."

She straightened. "Now, as for the two requests to dismiss the bond, denied. The occupation can be adjusted, but the bond itself will stand."

Two women at the back of the crowd slumped their shoulders.

"The request to create a human settlement within the city. Denied."

The folk who had come with that intent blinked in shock.

"Now, as for the nine who have arrived here and refused to work, you signed a contract. You acted of your own free will to leave a dying world, and you signed a contract to trade a portion of your lives for a chance at survival. You did not have to get on that shuttle, you did not have to take the education offered, and you certainly did not need to sign the final bond contract. This location was not your choice, but when you finish your bond, you can go where you like. Now, as for your refusal to work, that is easily dealt with, for three days'—four including today—refusal to work, you will have double shifts in the Mlia berry fields, harvesting the berries. I would warn you, the Mlia berries have a neurotoxic effect on humans. You will get aroused, your brain will overload, and you will die in a burning hell of your own making." She smiled tightly.

The crowd muttered darkly. She looked politely at them. "Did any of you have any genuine concerns?"

A young woman at the back of the crowd came forward. "Ma'am, the business that I was assigned to work for is a brothel. They keep trying to get me to act as a sex worker, even though I am just domestic service."

"That is something I can do something about."

"Oh sure, you know all about whoring."

The orb *cracked* down again. "Come here, Corporal. I have some questions for you."

He sneered and swaggered forward.

"What was my job on the day of impact?"

He puffed himself up. "You were the senator's whore."

"No, I wasn't even his employee. My boss was his assistant, and she died that day from the dust and gas in the air. I was trapped with a person I didn't know in a place I had no place being. I was an administrative assistant."

She looked at him again. "What did you have to pay to get your daily rations?"

He frowned. "They were issued to us."

"Who took them from you?"

"No one."

"Who beat you if you didn't follow orders? Who starved you? Which officers looked the other way so that they could use you, too? When did you have to start using your body just to get water?"

He blinked and backed up, the others in the room looked uneasy. "Sorry, Ma'am."

"So, when you sneer at my position, remember that here I am given what I need to live, I survive with the help from those around me, and none of them are humans. My own people believe me to be lowest of the low for simply surviving, but I am alive, and I am telling you all that you will abide by the terms of your bond, you will spread through the city and learn the ways of this society."

She smiled. "When you survive, and you can tell your children, and there can be children with the Idel. We are compatible. You will tell your children about how you survived your world, society, and home being destroyed and how you came out as proud citizens of a new world. They will tell their children, and the humans will make their way through history."

She sighed. "If we can survive here, and other humans can flourish on other worlds, we might just make it into the future in a way that no one could imagine. We can reach the future the long way around."

The humans weren't all happy, but after she got the particulars from the one young woman working in the brothel, she closed the session and got to her feet.

In a corner, the recorder got to his feet, and he smiled. "Excellent first session, Mistress. His lordship will have the data file within the hour."

She nodded. "Good. I hope to ratify that brothel incident this afternoon."

"You are doing it yourself, Mistress?"

"I am the current expert on a human with an alien-based sex life. I think I am qualified."

Her guards snickered.

The brothel discussion was a non-event. The owner had simply been trying to free the young woman of her bond as quickly as possible. She was young, exotic to the Idel, and could have paid off her bond in a week.

Fiona explained human ideas about sexuality and morality, and the brothel keeper nodded briskly. No further offers would be made. If the human changed her mind, she would have to initiate the conversation.

Fiona went over the details with Gwen, and once the girl understood, she was no longer nervous about returning to work, which had been very interesting and pleasant until the offer was made.

With her guards, she returned to the great house, and she found that she was rather smug.

In Aarak's office, he looked up and raised his brows. "You sent them to harvest Mlia?"

"Yeah, with a full warning. One week of doing that and they will return to work. Or, they will be transferred to the farms permanently. Either way, nobody shirks on my watch."

He came around the desk and hugged her. "It was a wonderful first try. I am very sorry about the water."

She blinked at him, and then, the reference clicked. "Well, it was stuff like that that drove me off my world and into your arms."

"Then, I am not quite as sorry." He grinned and leaned down to kiss her. "Only a hundred and fifty years to go."

She grabbed his hair. "But will you wear out first, or will I?"

Their kiss was a friendly battle, which turned into a friendlier wrestling match on the desk. It was an excellent end to a really good day.

Epilogue

Fiona walked through the fields of Ekadi, and she looked to the sky. It was nearly at the three-year mark, and the creature should be getting ready to return home.

Fiona closed her eyes and sent her thoughts to the sky. A moment later, she felt something in return.

She waited in the middle of the field, and after a few minutes, the huge creature appeared and approached.

When she was able to, she climbed the extended frond and settled on the dark-rainbow-hued skin. "Well, I just wanted to introduce you to my daughter. Balea, this is the creature of Ekadi.

When you next meet, you will be taller, and she will have a daughter of her own."

Her daughter waved her lime-green fists and sucked one of them. Her wings were tucked against her back, and the carrier that strapped her to Fiona kept her snug and safe.

Balea had been the product of eighteen months of gestation and a lot of apologies on the part of Aarak. She wasn't the first human-Hmrain cross-breed, and she wouldn't be the last.

The creature shared a giggling joy and flew them through the sky. Aarak was waiting until they passed over the city, and then, he would join them.

This part of the flight was just for the girls. They had earned it, after all.

Author's Note

Well, finally. *Lethal Impact* has made its appearance, and my brain seems to be coming back online after about eighteen months. Yay!

I am working on a third Shattered Stars book, but this one will be a little different.

Thanks for reading,

Viola Grace

About the Author

$\mathcal{V}$iola Grace (aka Zenina Masters) is a Canadian sci-fi/paranormal romance writer with ambitions to keep writing for the rest of her life. She specializes in short stories because the thrill of discovery, of all those firsts, is what keeps her writing.

An artist who enjoys a story that catches you up, whirls you around and sets you down with a smile on your face is all she endeavours to be. She prefers to leave the drama to those who are better suited to it, she always goes for the cheap laugh.